Watched

Also by Carol Chandler and published by Ginninderra Press
Black Mountain

Carol Chandler

Watched
and other stories

Acknowledgemens

An excerpt from *Watched* has previously appeared in *Four W*.

Watched and other stories
ISBN 978 1 76109 152 0
Copyright © Carol Chandler 2021
Cover photo by cottonbro from Pexels

First published 2021 by
GINNINDERRA PRESS
PO Box 3461 Port Adelaide 5015
www.ginninderrapress.com.au

Contents

Watched

Space seemed limitless since his release from prison. At the same time it threatened to dissolve his sense of self. It was better to stay in small areas. Tiny sections of his flat were more comforting and he'd cordoned them off, making them more restful. Sometimes he even slept in the car, drove somewhere away from the town, or parked near his building. The proximity and sensation of the car walls were reassuring. His jail cell was like that, simple white-tiled walls, a metallic toilet and basin; bed like a platform with a thin mattress, desk and TV.

As he drove towards Emilia's place, he wondered why she wanted to see him. He'd worked for her at the resort she owned and had a relationship before jail with her sister Tess. A branch leant across the path, light shimmering through the trees, an intense white and hazy. He parked the car and climbed out, glancing down below. The house was set back from the cliff, cantilevered, the walls of the balconies jutting out from the hillside. A wide sweep of bay led away to the mountains, their peaks a dull green in the distance. He could see the line of shops, the uneven buildings of the town reminding him of the high-rise tenements in the city, the heavy grumble of traffic drowning out words.

The darkness of the windows seemed to reflect light, flashes of silver, the slats of blinds half open. The door was a heavy wooden structure with gold ornamental knobs and swirls at the front, two rows of panels down the side. He glanced to his right at an insect buzzing through the trees and pulled back as he rang the bell.

After a few moments, Emilia appeared. She stood before him, dark, heavy lidded eyes, that strange twist of her mouth. She leant forward and kissed him and he recoiled a little, remembering how she wasn't to be trusted.

The interior had a large ceiling as they walked inside, wooden walls, a vase with the patterned flakes of lapis lazuli. In spite of falling on hard times, it was clear Emilia was still keeping up with appearances. As they walked through a doorway, a flash of white caught his eye, a child, malevolent-looking, like one of those imps you see in fairy tales. He was standing near the stairway and pulled away when he saw him. His skin was sickly and he turned back to Emilia but she said nothing.

Her own skin was pale, a hollow dip below the neck. She was wearing a dress draped loosely around her body, like a sarong, a pattern of batik crosses, a curious motif for a lapsed Catholic, a little like the twisted spikes on a barbed-wire fence.

Emilia walked past, leading him to another room. She turned to face him. Her eyes looked tired and he might have imagined it, but she seemed drunk.

'I'm glad you're back, Mick. It's been very difficult.'

He noticed again how her eyes were dark, rimmed with eyeliner, and that strange twisted mouth, uneven, a little hard, smeared with red lipstick. The sarong she was wearing was wrapped tight around her body, and she pulled at it, as if keeping herself together.

Turning to adjust the blinds, she swayed in front of him, the movement of her hips reminding him of Tess, the similarity between them. When she turned, he thought of her slim figure years ago. Her skin was burnt by the sun, a myriad of freckles tracing her arms. He remembered her lying by the pool with Tess, exchanging secrets, their silent laughter. They were like goddesses from another era, so different to where he'd come from.

'I'll explain, Mick. I heard you were going to see Tess. There's money missing from the resort.'

He noticed the blankness of her expression, as if she knew she'd said too much, a slight hint of cunning. She studied him and he realised that she probably didn't trust him, perhaps was just using him. He leant back on the couch awkwardly. She walked away from the window, a gentle rhythm to her step. There was something contained about her, not telling the truth.

'I can try and find out what's happening, Emilia, but I can't promise anything.'

'Good, do what you can. Tess isn't in a good way, that's what I heard. I think she's using again.' There was a hint of contempt in her tone.

The house was intimidating, a long staircase leading to an upper level. The child was on the stairs again. He glanced up at him, wondering who his parents were. The furnishings weren't really antiques, but made to look that way. He could see that more closely now. Emilia was clever with money, good at getting things to go a long way, that's what people had said, not as wealthy as you might think.

The walls had a tone of brown, as if they had been worn by the sun, fading, and he thought of Emilia's husband, John, a quiet man, melancholy, a bit depressive, like her mother.

'See what you can do, Mick. I feel like I've put a lot of time into it all and I'm weary. You should understand with your own background. Tess has something to tell you, anyway.'

He frowned at her, not liking this allusion to his past and lifestyle, conscious that she seemed to fiddle with the cross on a chain around her neck now like some kind of worry beads, as if she could transmit her anxiety to it. He wondered what it was that Tess had to tell him.

There was a large bookcase, cream couches, low beams in the ceiling, a vase with sprays of lavender. He sensed again that this was something of an illusion and he glanced at a mirror with golden spokes like the sun, the staircase disappearing to rooms upstairs. The child was still hovering at the top of the stairs and Emilia glanced up at him. He began crying in a mournful way.

He remembered the boulevard on the main drag, several levels looking out onto the beach, where tourists congregated, surfers riding the waves, families in clusters on the shore. It was where the resort she owned was situated and she often organised conventions for politicians.

Emilia studied him and he caught a glimpse of himself in the mirror, still the same swarthy complexion and black hair, brow furrowed, grooves down the side of his face.

'I heard you were doing well after your release from prison, Mick.'

He wondered if she was being sarcastic. Emilia smiled at him with an ironic look as if she knew all of this, knew that people were suspicious of him, had factored it all into the situation. She wasn't quite looking at him and he shifted a bit on her leather couch.

'Yeah, I learnt a lot in jail.'

She looked at him expectantly but he didn't say anything. He felt resentful, all this wealth they had, and remembered when they were even more well off. Tess was more eccentric then. There used to be paintings but they'd all gone.

When he turned back, he noticed a painting of Emilia on the wall. Her hair was swept back from her forehead and piled up in a beehive hairstyle, a headband with some spangles around it. There was a photo of her father, Simeon, on the buffet. He looked a little melancholy with secretive dark eyes, like Tess. His suit was rumpled around the edges. Usually he wore immaculate suits, so something looked wrong.

He could feel the resentment welling up in him again, the stress, unhappiness about his life. That's how they'd bonded, Emilia and himself. She was unhappy about her life too, even though they'd come from completely different backgrounds.

He looked again at the painting of Emilia on the wall. It was done a long time ago, another era, her figure curvaceous.

Emilia leant forward, looking strained. As he glanced at the painting, he noticed that her dark hair was swept away from a high forehead, her body tapering to a slim waist. The painting seemed to dominate the wall. He turned around and could see the bay in the distance through the trees outside. Emilia seemed unaware of the irony, a painting of her dominating the living room, assuming a larger presence than her own.

He remembered how she could be quite kind, would take in stray dogs and cats and help friends of the family. She'd felt sorry for him. He knew her stepfather had bullied her too, they'd bonded over that, and sometimes during his affair with Tess, he took it out on her, his frustration. Emilia had become nervous about it. It was then that she'd confided to him that her mother had also become an alcoholic. He glanced at her now and could see a resemblance to that younger woman in the painting, a distant innocence and girlishness that had all but vanished. There was a knowingness to her expression, but the painting had a lightness in the eyes, a vivacity which he no longer saw in Emilia. There was only the hardness of living. A type of Dorian Gray.

'A friend of mine painted it,' she said when she saw him looking at it.

At least she's lived life, he found himself thinking.

He glanced at the painting then back at her. 'I've never seen it before.'

'It's been in the cellar. I never bring it out.'

He caught himself frowning at her, thinking that he was being unfair. 'I've never seen it before,' he repeated.

'No, well, it's been stored away.'

She had a glint in her eyes now, and he shifted uncomfortably again.

The shadows of the rainforest seemed to brush the wall, a brown light, the room cavernous, a musky scent. He felt awkward as Emilia studied him. Her sarong had animals between the pattern of crosses, greens and browns like the room. She scrutinised him and he thought of the two sisters, the distance between them. In a way, he'd loved them both.

There was a noise outside; a mother and child fighting, screaming, perhaps the child on the stairs, and then the sound of hurried footsteps, someone scolding the child aggressively.

Emilia sighed and stood up. She left the room and he followed her, glancing into the dining room.

'See what you can do and let me know, Mick.'

He nodded and they walked to the door.

As he left the house, he glanced back at her. She was standing on the step studying a pathway that led back towards the hill. The garden seemed to disappear towards the bush, two rises like terraces, and then a flat smooth section, almost like a field, grasses that bent back in the wind towards a lawn higher up. Emilia paused for a moment, studying the grass before walking back inside. A large fence seemed to block off a building further up the hill, tall, with dark multiple-paned windows through the trees. He could see the small trail that Emilia had been looking at more closely now, leading away up the hill towards the house. The trail was worn away in the grass, like a pale piece of ribbon. He wondered who had been walking there, whether Emilia had used it. He remembered the child on the stairs, how strange he'd seemed.

As he walked towards the car, he sensed something behind him, and when he turned, a man stood near the trees, looking past him along the slope. The man moved away amongst the plants carrying an implement like a hoe, swinging it back and forth aggressively. His chin was pushed forward onto his chest and when he turned his heavy face appeared bloated and misshapen. His physique was powerful and his broad flattened features reminded him of someone he knew in prison. The guy used to pick on younger people but he'd managed to avoid him, because he'd used his wits to befriend powerful inmates. There was always something chilling about him. He had an arrogance and meanness that suggested he could stick a knife in you and twist it right up into your heart at the slightest provocation.

The car was in the driveway and he walked towards it, wondering who the man was in the trees, a gardener or perhaps a friend of Emilia's.

He climbed into the car and drove towards town, broken cliffs dipping below him to the sea. The road unfolded along the beach, past the fish shop with garish banners, a sign with a pale lotus, luminous points like a star. Restaurants had sprung up since he'd last been here before jail, an arcade with a Thai massage parlour.

The road led to a river further north. An island surrounded by mangroves beckoned across the water, spindly trees set back from the shore. A bike was tied up underneath the block of flats and he climbed out and walked towards the building.

The depressing interior hit him as soon as he walked inside, lino peeling near the door to the entrance, diamond pattern on the floor, mocking his attempts at change. The owner was letting the building run down before selling. He owned the entire block and was waiting for a developer, had no moral conscience about how his tenants were living and would no doubt try and claw some money back out of his bond. The lines in the lino reminded him of the bars in prison. He could see all the dirt between the creases. It seemed magnified, the filth building up, like the things that used to bother him in jail.

He walked into his flat, noticing the rusty light fittings, the silver tape at the entrance to the bathroom to stop a leak. It was similar to the tape wrapped around the blade of a knife he'd made which was hidden under the cushions of the couch. Sitting down, he tried to block it all out, the colour of a cushion, a deep crimson red like blood. A black scarf was draped across the couch, something he'd kept that no one knew about, another kind of keepsake from when things were more in control, nothing to do with the present, at least that's what he told himself.

He walked out to the balcony and looked down at Angela's flat below. She'd glanced up at him the day before as if she sensed something wrong. The corner of her flat was visible now, a glimpse of a small table, a wrought-iron chair, and a trail of bougainvillea. The darkness of the corner was just out of reach. She'd placed the table and two chairs in an orderly way and he wondered what kind of person she was, whether she had a partner or was alone. He remembered the greyness of his prison cell, how he was always on guard and then, something bright, a shiny star on a packet he'd kept, pathetic, but at the same time strangely meaningful.

The sandy flats of the river stretched away towards the sea, the ripples of the current flowing smoothly. It seemed to beckon, the river and the mangroves around the island. He watched the current ripple near the shore. A door had been pushed open downstairs, and what looked like hens scrabbled around in the yard. You could see through to the block next door. A woman joined a young girl, hanging up brightly coloured dresses. The child stood near her, holding on to her skirt. She shifted her position, holding her mother's hand. He watched the child closely before walking back inside. Sitting down on the couch, he felt the ridge of the knife under the cushion, the blade, sharp and metallic against his fingers.

Someone knocked at the door. It was Molly, the young girl from down the hall. She stared back with large dark eyes, body frail, matchstick thin, gangly arms and legs.

'What's the matter?' he asked gruffly.

Molly shifted her feet, staring back. He knew her mother, Yasmin, liked him because he'd helped rescue some of her things from Clinton, her ex-partner's, place.

Molly was still shuffling around and looked away, a hint of cunning in her eyes. 'Mum's making lunch. Do you want to come?'

'Yeah, okay,' he said, slouching back against the door.

Uncertain whether to go, he followed her down the hallway, curious why Yasmin had invited him. She greeted him at the door wearing her special occasion dress, a theatrical outfit, sewn from a filmy material daubed with fake jewels. Whenever she wore it, she seemed to glide down the street as if nothing touched her. Her slim build, dark eyes and cloud of hair gave her a fragile appearance, like one of those waif-like models that didn't really appeal to him.

The living room was draped with streamers. Some of them hung over a large photographic portrait of Molly's father, who seemed to look out at the world in a morose way. He'd been killed in a car crash and Yasmin had raised Molly by herself.

A heavy smell of tobacco drifted from another room and Angela, the woman from downstairs, walked in. He remembered the bougainvillea on her balcony, the carefully placed table, and the trails of blossoms that seemed to cascade from her flat to the one below. There was something at ease about her, a fluidity to her movements. She was wearing a dress of white cloth that made her look like a bride.

Angela glanced away quickly when she saw him looking at her. The way she retreated, a hesitation in her gaze, Yasmin must have said something. She frowned at him with washed-out blue eyes, a hint of disapproval on her face. Then he remembered Angela worked with Tess, his ex-girlfriend.

He was used to controlling things in prison and didn't like what was happening here, the position of Angela's table on the balcony and the orderly way she'd placed the chairs; something about her manner was troubling him.

Yasmin began talking about some fireworks at the bay, the spinning catherine wheels and rockets. It was as if he wasn't in the room. A dull resentment simmered and his mood began to sour. The way Molly moved her arms, whirling them like catherine wheels, put him on edge. Why had Yasmin invited him to lunch? The atmosphere shifted and Angela began talking about problems down at the local school, a kid who was acting strangely.

'What's he been doing?' asked Yasmin, sighing in an exasperated way.

'Punching people, spitting and making strange comments, a bit sexual, you know what I mean. He's Paul Donohoe's kid – well, his stepkid anyway.'

He flinched when she said Paul Donohoe. They'd had a long acquaintance before jail. 'Donohoe?'

'Yeah, he's with Suzanne. She does nothing with her kid. It's terrible what happened with her husband, Benjy. But you knew Benjy quite well, didn't you, Mick?' She turned to face him, a steely look in her eyes.

He frowned at her, thinking that she had to be watched. All they knew was that he'd been inside for armed robbery, nothing about Benjy's murder.

'Why is Paul with Suzanne?'

'It's because Benjy's gone.'

He was conscious of her bitchy tone, and wondered what was happening with Paul, why Suzanne had gotten involved with him. Paul had been a good friend of Benjy's. It was no surprise the kid was a mess if Paul was involved, but then, as he was Benjy's kid, it was no surprise either. Benjy had been living by himself when he'd killed him.

'I don't know what happened to Benjy,' he lied.

'Yeah, it was a while ago,' said Angela. 'He left but everyone knows he was killed.'

He was enjoying being ironic with her, watching her reaction, playing with them both. It was too big a temptation. They knew nothing about Benjy at all.

'I wonder why they split up,' said Angela. 'Suzanne's difficult too.'

'I heard he was living somewhere else for a while,' he said, playing with a fork on the table, standing it up, then flipping it around.

Angela's expression shifted slightly and he felt uncomfortable, thinking that she might know something. She stared at him and he glanced away, then he smiled slyly. She was leaning in her chair, studying him as if she wanted to say something but knew she shouldn't. She seemed unafraid of him now. He'd been conscious when listening to her that her voice had the same ironic tone he'd been using himself and he said nothing, annoyed that she seemed to be playing him at his own game.

'Tess hasn't been back long but she keeps to herself. No one knows what's happening with her.'

He studied her, conscious she was baiting him.

'I haven't seen her yet,' he said. 'I've only been here a few weeks.' Feeling irritated, he was going to get up and leave but then he remembered he was supposed to be staying for lunch. He watched Yasmin get up and move around the table as she served some food. Picking up his fork, he jabbed at the meat, putting it in his mouth. It was spicy, so different to the meals he'd eaten in prison.

'I've been thinking of setting up a stall at Manderley,' said Angela. 'Vintage stuff. You should look into it, Yasmin, selling stuff at the markets. Suzanne told me you used to sell pots.'

Yasmin's mood had changed. She seemed relaxed, eager to discuss day-to-day things.

He toyed with the food, not listening to them. He was thinking about Tess, what he was going to say to her, the way she'd been so upset the last time he'd seen her before jail.

'There's some good clothes there, and food,' Angela was saying.

They talked on about the markets but something had changed in Angela. She was looking at Yasmin from time to time as if she needed to get going.

'I might go up north sometime,' she said. She began describing the manta rays she'd seen on dives, the undulating movement of the rays and their barbed tails. There was a slight edge to her expression. She was beautiful if she scrubbed up a bit, pale skin, almond eyes and the tumble of dark curls around her face.

Yasmin looked a little flushed as if she'd been drinking and he noticed a wine glass nearby.

'I remember when you were last here, Mick,' said Yasmin.

He could tell she was aware of what was happening between him and Angela and didn't like it. Her voice was a little tense.

'You said you were looking for work. How long were you away?'

He glanced around, realising this was code for 'how long were you inside?' The euphemism irritated him. Molly had left the room and was in the bedroom.

'Five years.'

Her bright-eyed enthusiasm annoyed him, the slight sing-song tone in her voice. Angela was smiling as if she knew it too.

'Yeah, I don't like talking about the past,' he said, picking up on Angela's amused expression.

Her long graceful neck was slender but her lips were a little thin and sloped down slightly.

Yasmin glanced away. He'd been interested in her for a while but there could be nothing between them. She was too vulnerable.

'Yasmin, I'm sorry I can't stay. I have to meet someone at the bay.' He stood up, scraping his chair.

'Can I get a lift?' Angela asked. Her voice had a laconic tone but her eyes told a different story.

He remembered the ordered chairs and table on her balcony, the precision and tidiness. There was something calculating about her.

'Yeah, I have to see someone,' he said, curious why she was asking. 'But I can drop you down.'

He walked to the door, noticing a man down the hallway, hair curling across his forehead, eyes wide like a cat. The corridor was dark, a dusty alcove at the end, a door to a flat whose owner he was unfamiliar with. Torn fly strips were at the entrance, and an umbrella stand stood to the side with a design like a Chinese dragon.

He pulled out his car keys, turning back. Angela ignored him and began walking ahead. He studied the curves of her body, the pale shadows on her arms, something elusive about her, like a ripple in the waves.

'Who's that?' he asked, watching the man disappear down the hall.

'A friend,' she said, glancing back.

They walked downstairs and out to the road and he noticed the mangroves across the river. Angela walked towards the car. Her body reminded him of Tess and he began focusing on her.

They climbed into the car and he turned on the ignition. The ocean flickered as he drove through town, an intense blue, waves a delicate white on the crests. The movement of the car was relaxing, but the denseness of the crowds made him nauseous again.

Crowds of people were moving rapidly along the esplanade. An urge to get back to his room intensified or at least not get out of the car, but he kept driving towards the pub. People were standing nearby, milling around the entrance.

He glanced across at Angela and a clicking noise like cicadas distracted him as he climbed out of the car.

'I'll see you later, Mick,' she said.

He watched her walk in the direction of the marina, noticing the sway of her body again.

A woman sat near the entrance of the pub, dark matted hair, one arm heavily tattooed. Eaves overhung the porch, a row of kentia palms flanking the entrance.

A crowd of drinkers overflowed into the street, seagulls squawking near the tables. The bitter smell of beer drifted out from the public bar as the din of people and voices pushed towards him. Feeling queasy, he steadied himself against the wall. He pulled himself up and stared out across the crowd, noticing a man with a stubbly beard, tall, heavy-set. The man looked familiar, sharp face, high cheekbones. In some ways he resembled himself, dark, swarthy complexion, slim build, although the man's physique was a little heavier, more muscular.

Unnerved by the resemblance, he glanced away. The fronds of ferns fluttered in the breeze of a ceiling fan. He stared across at a white timber balcony that overlooked the street, wondering why the man was watching him, an odd reflection of himself staring back.

A vine had woven its way through the heavy green netting so that the occupants of the beer garden were partially hidden from view, their skin appearing dusky and cool in the dappled shade of the leaves. Lyle, a friend from before jail, was supposed to be meeting him but there was a message from him on his phone saying he'd see him later.

The air was fresh when he walked outside, but the smell of the sea had a salty tang. It mingled with the pungent smell of diesel oil from a large fishing trawler. The sound of jackhammers reverberated in the distance as he walked along the beach.

A line of shops stretched away like a carnival as he walked inside the dark air-conditioned chill of the marina arcade. The shop that sold tours to the islands was decked out with fluorescent purple, lime green and hot lolly-pink coral, as well as tanks of brightly coloured fish. Next door, a giant fibreglass shark hung at the entrance to the surf shop. Its large triangular teeth and beady black eyes loomed out of the darkness, menacing passers-by. The windows of the gift shop were lined with iridescent paua shells and brightly coloured stones fashioned into earrings and bracelets. The blue and green surfaces of the paua shells were brilliantly polished so that they glistened like stars on the surface of a pool. Running his fingers over the different surfaces as he always did, like a ritual, he studied the facets of the crystal. They were hard and cold against his fingertips like glass.

He picked up a piece of rose quartz. It was something that Tess would like, marbled, like the rosy hues in the sand further north. It felt warm to touch. Clenching the stone in his hand, he studied the reflections in the light. That image of a mirror returned, watching himself with a woman. Putting the stone back down, he left the shop.

He walked towards a white weatherboard church that stood at the end of the park. The sky and sea were visible but the sight of the sea made him nervous, the undulating movement of the ocean. When he walked inside the church, someone had placed a tiny vase of purple blossom in a corner, flowers trailing gently towards the floor. It reminded him of Angela's bougainvillea on her balcony, the delicate trail of petals. He tried to imagine her here in her white dress with the gold thread sitting in the church like a bride.

The chapel was simple, like something that had existed thousands of years ago, not the false building that he'd found himself in as a child. A woman was sitting on one of the pews. She was older, probably around the same age as his mother. Walking to the window, he watched the ocean moving, a vivid field of blue against a paler strip of sky. An odd moment of tranquillity took hold as he stared out through the window, but then the niggling restlessness returned that had dogged him since jail, like a crab scrabbling out from its hole. Turning back, he noticed the woman staring at him, her eyes wide. She turned away quickly.

The sun's powerful rays hit his back as he walked outside, burning into him, shirt sticking slightly to his body.

A lonely fossicker bent down to pick up shells. He remembered the paths criss-crossing near Benjy's, and the area where he'd walked to the rocks. No one knew about Benjy's murder, only about the armed robbery.

Climbing into the car, he drove along the coast road to Tess's. Cliffs sloped down to the sea, pinnacles emerging from the waves. They'd broken with a splashing sound when he'd stood at the edge, a thwack against the surface.

The road led through bush, rocks disappearing into a gully. Tess's place was up ahead, long white walls, banana palms to the side. Parking the car, he climbed out and walked towards the building, a series of wide steps, doors with gold bands across them. He rang the doorbell and after a few moments, Tess appeared, her dark eyes, guarded.

'Come in, Mick.'

Her voice sounded flat and he glanced to the right at a room full of boxes as he followed her down the hall. It was obvious she'd been unpacking. She'd only been back a few weeks. He'd only been back three weeks himself and it was taking time to get his bearings. The corridor led to a large living room which opened out onto a balcony. The room was lighter than the rest of the house, ceiling high, walls painted white. A glass door opened out onto the veranda. Polished floors reflected the light cast by an antique light fitting. Tess sat down in a cane chair opposite.

There was still something between them, he could sense it. They'd cut off contact when he went to jail but she'd written just before his release. Something was weighing on her mind, she said, but she refused to elaborate. Tess was staring at him awkwardly now. She'd been overseas for most of the time he'd been in jail.

'Mick, a man came here today. He was asking about Benjy.'

The darkness of the rocks came into his mind and the moon on the surface of the water. He'd been distracted, and leant back on the couch, trying to compose himself as soon as she mentioned Benjy. He wondered if she suspected him.

'He knows Benjy's family.' Her expression was cold.

A dog barked outside and light streamed through the glass like a golden beam.

'Remember Benjy was suspected of abusing that girl.'

Palm trees touched the side of the house, fronds visible near the wall. Something had changed in her and the muscles around his back tensed. The lines of her face were the same, the delicate nose, slightly tilted, dark eyes, but her cheekbones were more pronounced, cadaverous.

'Well, the mother was a friend of Emilia's, wasn't she? Why don't you ask her?'

He noticed an easel in the corner. It reminded him of the story of

Dorian Gray and the painting back at Emilia's place. Tess had told him about Dorian Gray, a man who remains eternally young while his sins are transferred to his portrait. He realised now that he'd first seen the painting of Emilia many years ago. When he'd first seen it, he'd thought Tess had painted it, a kind of joke on Emilia. Tess had always wanted to be an artist but a lack of self-belief and practicalities had gotten in the way. Emilia was older, a businesswoman and more successful. They were half-sisters, different fathers, just as he and his brother were half-brothers, but Emilia didn't seem to have aged in the painting. She looked confident and younger than Tess, more self-assured.

'No, I didn't paint it,' Tess had said sarcastically when he'd mentioned it. 'So you think she doesn't seem to have aged in the painting?'

He remembered the disdain in her voice. 'I always thought you were talented, both in music and art,' he said, watching her glance towards the door. 'Are you working at your art? Emilia's worried about you. She said there was some money missing at the resort.'

'I don't have time these days and I don't know anything about the money either. I heard about it but she knows I had nothing to do with it.'

She said it abruptly and he realised she'd asked nothing about himself. An emptiness crept up on him. She probably thought he wasn't worth it and wanted to draw a line under things. He'd let her down and she was keeping him at arm's length, punishing him. That's what was behind it. They came from different backgrounds and she'd tried to help him, Emilia too, but he'd let them both down.

She looked at him evasively and that feeling of envy niggled at him, the fact that they'd had a privileged upbringing, private schools, swimming pools. He stared back at her, wondering if she was mocking him, because she still looked a little contemptuous. The palm tree was clearly visible through the window, its branches fanning down in the breeze. He studied it and remembered how well off they were, and how they liked beautiful things, flashy ornaments, nice houses.

'The guy, I mentioned, who was asking about Benjy. He knows Benjy's family.'

He sat up stiffly on the couch.

'There's nothing strange about it, Mick. Why are you reacting like that? I just thought you'd want to know. I mean people have been asking about Benjy for some time. His family want closure.'

'Closure? Why doesn't the guy ask Lyle? He had more to do with him than me.'

His eyes narrowed, thinking about Lyle, remembering how the police had interviewed him about Benjy's disappearance. He and Lyle had worked together.

'He should talk to Lyle,' he said crankily. 'Xanthe, the kid's mother, told me about the abuse, by the way. She said Benjy had done it. You remember how people were talking about it. He spent a lot of time with the girl.'

Tess shifted slightly in her seat and leant back. 'That's not what I heard. I heard it was a misunderstanding. Anyway, the guy did speak to Lyle. The family want to find out what happened.'

'What's the guy's name?'

'Brandt.'

He reached over to some cashews on the table, crunching into them; thinking about the kid he'd seen at Emilia's when he'd visited earlier. He'd seemed a little restless, a ghostly image. There was a point when he'd moved closer and noticed dark circles beneath the boy's eyes. He was in another room, and seemed to be hiding from him, but at the same time he'd glanced at him knowingly. Then he remembered himself at that age. He'd been sick, and his stepfather hated him, thought he was weak. His own demeanour had been unpleasant. It had gotten worse under his stepfather's bullying, but at the same time he was vulnerable and lost.

'So this guy who was asking about Benjy?' he asked, trying to compose himself. 'What does he want?'

'I don't know, just to find out what happened. There was something missing from the house, a statue.'

He frowned when she mentioned the statue, thinking that was all they were interested in, nothing to do with Xanthe's kid or the abuse. He'd taken the statue after he'd killed Benjy. He glanced around the room. There was something illusory about the place, a brittleness, similar to Emilia's place. He wasn't going to tell Tess anything. She probably suspected him but what was she holding back on herself?

There was a telescope silhouetted through the window on the porch, the ghostly reflections of the glass ball swinging back and forth in the net. He could tell she didn't trust him, all these objects in the house he didn't recognise, the telescope, a child's toy. What was it, some kind of spider or a praying mantis made of plastic?

'The guy who came here, Mick, he's here for a while. Did you know Seth saw someone in the distance the night Benjy disappeared? He was staying with Suzanne and went to see Benjy.'

'What, Benjy's kid? He and Suzanne had nothing to do with Benjy. I heard Suzanne's with Paul Donohoe now.'

'Well, Seth was there. He didn't end up going to the house. He walked down from Suzanne's and then saw something. He was too scared to go further. He did say something but he was too afraid to talk to the cops. You know how they are.'

He had a sense she'd wanted to say something more but had lost her nerve, maybe something about Seth. Seth wouldn't have seen anything. There was no one around when he'd been there.

Standing up, he walked outside to the balcony, troubled about Seth. Tess walked out too, standing there stiffly by the doorway. She smiled at him when he turned, perhaps because she was safely at a distance, he didn't know, or it might be that she knew there was that attraction between them, and felt it herself.

'Mick I have to get ready for work. We can talk later. They called me in unexpectedly. Someone's sick.'

He watched her walk back and pause for a moment.

'Okay,' he said crankily. 'Yeah, I'd like to talk to you more.'

She walked with him outside, bending forward and hugging him, the warmth of her body reassuring. He glanced back towards the series of wide steps and the doors with gold diagonal bands set across them. The bands seemed to fortify the door, keeping people out.

Climbing into the car, he began driving back along the highway, thinking of Seth, Benjy's son. It was most likely Lyle who had been at the house if that's who he thought he saw when he walked down. Seth was afraid of him too. That's why he hadn't talked. Benjy had aggravated people higher up, 'a self-cleaning oven', the cops had said. They didn't really care what had happened with his disappearance. It was one less criminal to worry about. Their suspicion had always been on Lyle and no one knew what had happened with Benjy because no body had been found.

The church looked tiny as he drove past and he remembered the woman he'd seen in the morning, how she reminded him of his mother, that aloof unpleasant gaze. The church was set back in a wide expanse of green, the pale stretch of sand and ocean behind it.

The doors on the balcony of Angela's flat glinted in the sunlight as he arrived back, curtains pulled across the glass. He climbed out of the car and walked towards the building. The door creaked open and he climbed the stairs. There was a knowingness about Angela he didn't like, as if she knew all about him and was just waiting for him to put a foot wrong. Opening the door to the flat, he walked into the bedroom. Studying a pattern of gold flowers on the wall, he wondered if Benjy and Angela were connected. He wracked his brain trying to think if Benjy had ever mentioned her. His bedroom was more pleasant than the living room with the grey carpet, the same as prison, the suffocating closeness of the walls.

The room looked lighter as he lay down and relaxed further into the mattress but that image of Benjy's body began to intrude into his consciousness. He twisted around to look out towards the balcony.

Pigeons cooed on the ledge outside the window, light streaming through a lattice on the chair. The noise in his head seemed to intensify. Trying to relax, he looked up at the torn curtain, thinking of Yasmin's filmy dress.

There was a knock at the door and he got up to answer it. It was

Yasmin's daughter, Molly. She was standing in the doorway, staring up at him. He remembered how he'd helped rescue some of their things from Clinton, Yasmin's ex's place. That's why they trusted him.

'Mum's crying.'

'I'll come later,' he said irritably. 'I'm busy.'

Molly looked upset and he relented, walking down to Yasmin's. She was sitting in the kitchen with her head in her hands.

'Mick, the police picked Clinton up,' she said, glancing up at him. 'There's never any evidence. It's all threats and he's clever. Even when there's evidence, they do nothing.'

'I can't do much, you know that. I'm on parole.' He looked around the flat at the shabby scalloped lines on the wall, the powder-blue paint, and the window that looked out onto the lawn.

Yasmin seemed to relax but, at the same time, she looked frightened. He wondered if she was self-medicating as she picked up a bottle and poured herself some wine. The whooshing da da beat of samba music distracted him through the window. It skipped and pulsed through the air, a gallop of notes jumping, and then a gentle gliding pulse. For a moment, he felt anxious, wondering if it was coming from Angela's flat.

Yasmin offered him some wine. He took it, maintaining a distance while still present, following her words as she began talking about Clinton.

'He was a good man once,' she said. 'But he's changed.'

He pulled back, not liking the discussion. It was ridiculous to think Clinton had been a good man.

Her skin was smooth but a little flushed with the wine. He could see he'd unsettled her and smiled back, hoping she'd relax. Yasmin's words were coming fast, in short bursts jumbled together, crammed in on each other. He could barely take in what she was saying, but knew that she was anxious, because this was how it always was, her tone rushed, voice excited and resonant. Suppressing his irritation, he decided to indulge her because in amongst the chatter there were tiny gems of wisdom and observation, glittering comments that caught his attention, scattered amongst the sands of anxiety and fear.

Glancing up at the walls, he noticed the blue and white scalloped lines again, a small star that Molly had drawn on a piece of paper from a picture he'd shown her. Yasmin had originally wanted to call Molly Umiko, child of the sea.

'You should get away from Clinton,' he said. 'You said he'd changed.'

'It's becoming more difficult. He was different once. I don't like leaving Molly with him, but he was a good man for many years.'

He snorted when she said Clinton was a good man. Some salad sat on the table. The rocket's delicate leaves reminded him of the bracken that lined the creek beds at his childhood home, the whipping and cracking sound of birds. He remembered his stepfather's bullying tone, the incessant clicking of the beaded fringe strips that separated his own room from his mother's bedroom. His stepfather had taken him in after his mother left.

'Yasmin, have you ever done something you really regret?'

She looked at him patiently, waiting for him to explain, but he said nothing, only smiling at her cryptically. Conscious of her anxious look, he remembered the screeching of bats in the fig trees at his childhood home, the remoteness of the bushland paths and the sulphurous colour of the hills.

A small spider caught his eye in the corner, and he watched its web floating freely, dangling in space, swaying crazily back and forth, like a pendulum.

Yasmin hesitated as if she wasn't taking him seriously and he frowned, watching her purse her lips.

'What do you mean?'

'Nothing,' he said. 'Maybe it's the real Clinton you're seeing now. Have you ever thought of that? I'll come and get you if you want to go to Roland's party. Let me know if you have any more problems. I'll go and see Clinton, see what I can do.'

She looked away, unsettled by his tone. Her hair brushed past her shoulders lightly like a cloud.

He stared at her, annoyed that she wanted something done about Clinton but at the same time didn't appear to trust him.

Yasmin pushed her hair back with her hands.

'Are you still working at the resort?'

'Yeah,' she said, looking nervous.

He reached over to the wine glass on the table, taking a swig. 'I'll come and get you later. Or come down when you're ready.'

He walked down to his flat. Stepping out onto the balcony, he stared out across the mangroves, towards a house on the other side. A man sauntered towards the wharf with what looked like a bucket and a fishing line. He jumped down onto the sand, walking towards the shoreline. There was something carefree about his movements, something he missed.

Moving back inside, he noticed the black scarf again. The material was delicate with streaks of gold thread, and he looped it through his hands, remembering that game he'd played with Tess. Putting the scarf down, he pulled out some tools from the cupboard, examining the point of the spanner.

Walking downstairs to the car, he opened the bonnet, tinkering with the engine, the nuts and bolts. He liked the way it all fitted together, nothing out of place, nothing unexpected.

Glancing back towards the flats, he noticed Angela on the balcony. He remembered how he'd tightened the scarf around Tess's neck till she blacked out, then released it, that sense of control. Angela looked attractive, her willowy figure, the way she was leaning forward on the railing. He already knew she and Tess worked together but they were in different sections at the resort.

The river flowed past the island, the ripples of the current moving slowly. He watched the movement of the current, thinking about Angela and then the scarf. Walking towards the building, he glanced up to see if she was still there but she'd gone. A door on a loose hinge under the building creaked at the side as he pushed it back. Nothing inside, only the darkness, a rustling sound like a rat.

Moving back to the car, he worked on the engine for a while, then he returned inside.

Yasmin's face had an odd passivity when she'd been speaking, pared down. He hadn't felt anything when she'd been talking about Clinton, something dead inside him, something from the past. The door was slightly ajar, the kitchen to his left, and he fixed himself a drink, and watched TV, before getting ready for the party.

Yasmin appeared at his door in the evening. She'd changed into a lacy blue top that flattered her fragile face, and dark eyes. He wondered where Molly was.

'I don't know if this party's going to be any good,' he said abruptly. 'I haven't seen Roland for a while.'

'He's changed, keeps to himself, doesn't get involved with Lyle and Paul.'

'Really?' he said, doubting this was true. 'Do you know anything about a guy who's been asking about Benjy? Brandt's his name. He saw Tess.'

Yasmin looked puzzled. 'Oh yeah, Brandt,' she said at last. 'Angela knows him. He was staying with her.'

He remembered the guy he'd seen earlier in the hallway, his athletic build, the way he'd studied him before turning away.

Yasmin picked up her bag. She moved slightly away from him.

'Who is he?'

'Someone connected with Benjy's family. He worked for them.'

They walked downstairs and he climbed into the car, bothered by the poinsettia petals that dotted the road, trailing near the gutters, like stains of blood.

'How well do you know Angela?'

'Not that well.'

'I thought you knew her well.'

'Just from the resort. She's hard to get to know. I start to think I know her, then I don't.'

'What does that mean?'

'She's kind of private. It's hard to explain. She's quite outgoing but she keeps to herself.'

He clicked his tongue impatiently, thinking this was stupid. 'She seems kind of pushy to me, the way she looks at you.'

'No, she's got a lot of different sides.'

'What do you mean?' he said scornfully. 'What did you hear about Brandt?'

Yasmin pulled back from him, looking nervous. 'He worked with her in a bar. It was before I came here. Benjy used to buy drugs from Lyle, but Benjy wasn't involved in the same things. He helped a lot of people. His family want to know what happened to him. He could be kind to people.'

'Kind to people!' he snapped. 'He did nothing for anyone. How can you say that?'

'You didn't know him, Mick.'

Swinging around, he noticed her flinch slightly. Bristling at Yasmin's comments, he started the car and drove through town. What did she mean 'Benjy was kind to people'? Had he missed something? He didn't think so.

A large brick building loomed in the distance, looking down towards the bay. Glancing back down the road at a path that led through bush, he remembered the cliffs, and platform with dark pools, how he'd stood very close to the edge, staring down below. He wondered if it was a lie about Benjy, that he'd gotten it all wrong, that Xanthe had manipulated him somehow about the abuse, but he didn't think so.

'Did Angela say anything about Ruby, Xanthe's daughter, the girl Benjy was supposed to have abused?'

Yasmin turned to look at him. 'No, she didn't.'

He pulled over at an entrance, feeling troubled. Xanthe didn't know about his own background but she'd deliberately told him about Ruby, perhaps hoping he'd react.

The door to Roland's had a large architrave, palm trees towering above it in the moonlight. It reminded him of a painting back at

Emilia's, not the Dorian Gray one, another one with a tunnel and figures moving along it, ghostly shadows curling like tongues of smoke. The figures seemed to be pulled forward towards a destination not of their own making. The noise in his head seemed to intensify again and he tried to calm himself down. Tess had commented once that Roland and his family were different to other people. His mother used to clean houses like this.

He climbed out, staring up at the house, his heart beating quickly. They walked inside together but Yasmin walked into a room at the side, while he continued on down the hallway, looking for Roland. He'd worked for him on one of his building projects when he'd first come here.

The door was embossed with white panels, a long white wall, like a tunnel, leading to a living room. Glancing through a doorway, he noticed a man on a couch, his large belly rotund like a pregnant woman. The man glanced up as he leant towards a bowl, ignoring him.

He walked out to the balcony. Some mellow jazz drifted from inside as he sat down on a cane chair near the railing, leaning towards the edge. The estuary was wide and the tide covered the flats that were exposed in daylight. A woman stood nearby, bangles with plastic fish jangling on her arms, green, red and gold. He watched the flick of the fishes' tails and remembered the fish shop where he'd been in the morning before he'd gone to Emilia's, a whale trapped in the river, how they couldn't get it out, people standing on the banks. The sound of plastic fish jangled on the woman's arms.

The lights of the marina were in the distance, twinkling, the water smooth, reflective. He stared out at the bay. There was an old fibro house built on besser blocks next door, timber leadlight portions of a building. It was relaxing, sitting there. People were talking, a woman and a man, standing near the doorway. The man had his back to him.

'He must have been hurt badly,' the man said. 'You wouldn't want to cross him.'

He wondered who they were talking about. Maybe Lyle. He was like that, people were afraid of him.

The music was like the melody back at the apartment, slow and passionate. Yasmin was in the centre of the floor, dancing, swaying in circles, stepping swiftly back and forth, sensual and relaxed. He'd never seen her that way before. There was almost a sense of abandonment about her. She was with a man and he didn't like the way the guy was leaning towards her. He seemed unworthy of her, no class.

The ghostly reflections of the window on the porch distracted him, something swinging back and forth in a net. He thought he saw something flying and glanced around quickly, something swift, a bird or bat.

There was a room down the hall and he left the balcony and walked towards it. His body tensed as soon as he entered. Angela was sitting there. Her black dress touched the floor as she leant back on a couch. He caught a glimpse of her legs, toenails painted red. Her hair had a strange reddish tint and the tumble of dark curls around her cheeks, made her appear beautiful. He stared at her admiringly in spite of himself. The pink stone he'd seen at the marina came into his mind. Angela didn't deserve something like that.

He studied her face, eyes almond-shaped, and glanced back towards the hallway to see if he could see Yasmin, some kind of anchor against Angela's unpleasantness.

'I was at Paul and Suzanne's,' Angela said.

As soon as she mentioned them, he knew they'd been talking about him. He leant forward as if to intimidate her, but she didn't react.

'Seth saw something at the house. They're worried about him.'

'Benjy's kid?'

'Yeah.'

He sat down, conscious she was baiting him. 'Yeah, I heard that. Probably Lyle. I heard he'd already talked to people.'

Angela's expression didn't change. She stared back at him and his mind began to wander, trying to connect all the pieces. It was probably Lyle. He'd visited earlier. They knew nothing about Benjy or what had happened. He never touched drugs himself but Benjy and Lyle did. They were both connected. Lyle was into everything and had contacts overseas. He had dark hair, similar to Benjy. They could all easily be mistaken but then Benjy didn't sell drugs, only Lyle did. Benjy was only a part-time user. He remembered the burnt, charred smell of meat wafting towards him as he'd approached the house, how Benjy had a barbecue earlier with Lyle.

'I don't know what happened,' he said. He reached over and extracted a cigarette from a packet on the table. 'Seth's a strange kid. He probably saw Lyle. He was there earlier.'

'That's what the cops think,' said Angela. 'Seth was confused about the time. Benjy's mother's very sick.' She seemed to back down and looked distressed.

He leant back, surprised. What did he care about Benjy's mother?

'Seth's a handful,' he said. 'I heard Tess was with Joss Cameron. You know, that guy who manages the nightclub.'

'Yeah, he's a nice guy. She's not with him, though.'

He frowned, not liking the implication that Joss was more worthy of Tess than himself, but glad Tess wasn't with him. He reached over to an ashtray, wondering what Angela was thinking.

'There was a kid at Emilia's,' he said, remembering the boy he'd seen there. 'Do you know who he is?'

'Benjy's mother has cancer. Did you know that?'

He frowned; annoyed she was changing the subject away from the boy. He didn't care about Benjy's mother. He just wanted to know what Angela was hiding and who Tess was involved with.

'His mother wants some resolution to the whole thing.'

'Resolution?' He leant back on the couch and wondered how well Angela knew Benjy.

Her eyes were sullen. She reached over to a frangipani on the table and twisted it with her fingers, the delicate tips, twisting the flower back and forth. The heavy scent of the flower was distracting.

'I heard some people out on the balcony,' he said. 'They were talking about someone. It sounded like a fight.'

'Yeah, at Tanglewood. I don't go there any more.'

Angela stared at him unhappily and he realised he'd sounded callous about Benjy's mother and her cancer.

'It must have been hard on Benjy's mother,' he said, trying to appear concerned. 'I didn't know she had cancer.'

She nodded, staring back at him. 'Benjy pissed people off in the city. They all knew each other there, Lyle, Benjy. I only knew them here but Benjy wasn't really involved. He just fell in with the wrong crowd.'

That's all they cared about, not the abuse of Xanthe's kid, nothing else, and probably the statue he'd taken. He studied Angela, wondering why she'd fallen for the idea that Benjy was an innocent person.

'I know you ended up committing that robbery because of debts,' Angela said, leaning back. 'That's why you went to jail, wasn't it? I heard about your stepfather. He sounds like he was a hard man. Tess told me about him.'

As soon as she mentioned his stepfather, he tensed up. Angela appeared to smile slightly. She continued smiling at him and he felt uncomfortable, thinking of his stepfather, how he'd been kind to him at the start, taken him in after his mother left. He didn't think she knew anything and wondered if Dan, his brother, had said anything to her. Dan didn't want anyone to know about it either, the things his stepfather had done, but he had to protect himself. He didn't care if anything happened to him. People had even said Dan had killed Benjy and he'd never contradicted it. It was a kind of game. Dan had never protected him. So why should he care? They could focus on him. He'd only come back to see if Tess wanted to leave and knew his brother was frightened of him.

Angela's face was directly in front of him, and he had a feeling that if he pushed her, she would crumple into nothing. She flinched a little and he stared at her, leaning back on the couch. Angela sat back as he brooded about his stepfather and his brother. She looked seductive, the way she was leaning, her slender neck and body. The resentment churned inside him, thinking about it all and he felt drawn to her, as he glanced up at a photo on the wall. Angela was attractive, even though he disliked her. Then he remembered Yasmin's strange comments about not really knowing Angela, that she had many sides and was private. He pulled away from her.

'Yasmin seems to like you,' he said, trying not to sound sarcastic.

She said nothing, a slight smile on her lips. He wondered what she was thinking, if she was picking up on all the contradictions. But why was she so interested?

That unpleasant memory returned of his stepfather, and he turned quickly, glancing back at Angela.

'What's the matter?'

'Nothing,' he said calmly.

'Tess is worried about you.'

'Yeah, why?'

'She's worried how you're settling in after jail.'

He grunted when she said this and remembered the child through the doorway at Emilia's, a flash of white, malevolent-looking. He was glaring at him. He sensed the child was doomed like himself and wondered who he was. There was something strange about him.

'That kid at Emilia's.'

Angela shifted back in her seat. 'I think Benjy was okay, Mick,' she said, ignoring him. 'There's been all this talk about people misunderstanding things with that other kid, Ruby. It wasn't true that he did things to her. I heard she was coached by her mother.'

His eyes narrowed as she said this. 'I think it was true. I know the sort of guy Benjy was. He was guilty of plenty of things.'

'Yeah, but that doesn't make him a paedophile.'

He stared back. 'Just the way he acted with Ruby, something weird about it.'

'I think people have been wondering about it.'

He glared back at her, wondering if Angela was suspicious of him and thought he might have done it himself. He began thinking about the other kid at Emilia's, bothered by him, his pale skin and surly look. Angela bit her lip and looked annoyed. Was this other kid connected with Ruby?

'Yasmin said something similar,' he said. 'That Benjy wasn't guilty, that Xanthe made it up about touching Ruby.'

He felt something slipping from his grasp. The same man he'd seen earlier at the pub was near the doorway, dark, high cheekbones, similar to himself. He was watching him and that unpleasant sense of foreboding took hold. He brushed it aside, a sense that things were about to crack. Feeling hemmed in, he knew he wasn't going to get anything more out of Angela. He sensed it, the way she was looking at him. It was obvious she thought he wasn't to be trusted.

'I'm going to find Roland,' he said angrily. He stood up and left the room.

As he walked outside, looking for Roland, he noticed the pool. Bending down towards a leaf, he felt hemmed in again as he watched it float, suspended on the water. Poinsettia petals streaked the ground, blood-red in the moonlight. He stared down at them. The water was slightly murky, but at the same time shining in the light, beams flickering across the surface. Tess had grimaced when he'd told her about the dirty pool, the fact that they were rich and didn't clean it. It was a type of decadence, she said, like her parents. He remembered feeling resentful too, as if Tess had brought something out in him, cleverly directing it away from herself. It was around the time he'd discussed Benjy and his stepfather with her, how they were similar. Tess hadn't agreed with him and he'd gotten angry with her. He glanced back at the house, thinking that he saw himself as some kind of protector of children, but it wasn't true. He wasn't really a protector. He was a sham.

He needed to see his brother and walked across the lawn. Poinsettia trees leant gracefully across the grass, red flowers contrasting with the green in the pool, traces of moss and leaves at the bottom. He wondered why they cared so little about the place, Tess had also said they were recluses, strange people who cared little about the opinion of others. He liked that at first, the fact that they didn't care about people's opinions but then Tess said there was a type of meanness in it. It had troubled him at the time. He didn't know what she meant. The patterns of leaves in the pool were speckled like meandering paths. He studied the way they led to the steps, the confusing changes in direction. His mother had cleaned places like this.

He was distracted, watching the pool, thinking of his mother, how she'd left them, abandoned him and his brother. There was a stiffness in his spine, as he turned and walked along the road towards the car, a sense of resolve, noticing lights hovering indistinctly in the distance. He wondered what had happened to her. Troubled by the memories that were beginning to creep into his mind, he glanced up at a steeply wooded hillside on the right.

Something brushed his arms as he walked towards the car, and he flinched, the sensation of dead skin again, the coldness of a lifeless body, his stepfather grabbing him, pushing him down. A man walked along the road towards him, jowly, black hair plastered across his scalp. He recognised him as Justin, a friend of Roland's, and nodded at him as he passed by, dark face beneath a hood, half beard visible on his narrow chin. He turned and stared at him as he walked towards the end of the road, walking quickly to the corner.

Towards the end of the street, a strange light flickered, the distant shapes of trees. He remembered the warmth of Tess's body, and the softness of her skin, her glazed look, how he couldn't bear to look at her.

He was distracted momentarily as he climbed into the car. Turning on the ignition, he drove for a while, pulling up near a hill. He climbed out, walking down to the beach. Walking along the sand, he climbed up onto a rock platform. It sprawled away from the base of the cliff, like a magnificent stage, covered in dozens of tidal pools, shining like small mirrors in the moonlight. Towards the end of the platform, the waves rose up in curtains of spray. He stood there, watching the way they hit the rocks, thinking about how he'd struggled with Benjy.

There was a man fishing near the waves. A night fisher. He studied the slim line of his body, the way he raised his arm and flung the line into the water, his strong physique. An unpleasant memory returned of his stepfather, standing there on the rocks, how he'd forced him back into a sandhill.

He walked up the hill away from the beach, bothered by his thoughts, conscious of the water, smooth like glass, and the waves rising up. In some ways, Benjy was similar to his stepfather. That's what he told himself. It made sense what he'd done then. Benjy was a liar too, the facade of a good guy, at least that's what he thought.

Climbing into the car, he turned on the ignition, driving along the streets. There was an ordered geometry to the houses, a weatherboard set back from the road, a porch with a worn settee, and a rolled-up piece of netting. It reminded him of his stepfather's place, the rickety veranda and the gaps between the planks.

He pulled up in town and bought some cigarettes, noticing a man walking past a shop. His shoulders were hunched. The collar of his cream trench coat was turned up like a spy. It covered the back of his neck like camouflage, a barrier against the world. He watched him walk to the shop window, clutching a piece of paper and some masking tape. People turned slightly to stare at him. He stuck something on the window, then walked into an alley near the arcade.

Walking back to the car, he passed by a small park with winding paths, shaded by day with plants and ferns. When he glanced down, he noticed a ten-dollar note on the ground. Bending over, he clutched the note, shoving it in his pocket. Climbing into the car, he drove further south towards his brother's.

A private wharf jutted out from the river, a patio with palms in bronze pots, that looked down onto the yard of his brother's block of flats. Climbing out, he walked to the entrance and rang the bell. After a moment, his brother replied through the intercom. He pushed the door open and climbed the stairs.

Carly, his brother's girlfriend, was on the couch in the living room. Her hair was dyed an auburn colour and her expression was trance-like, arms misshapen beneath her top. Knick-knacks were scattered about the room, vases, ornaments and carvings.

'Dan told me he's getting rid of them,' Carly said, gesturing towards all the objects.

He glanced around at the cheesecloth curtains, the electric insect zapper in the corner. The room had dark panelled walls, plants by the side.

Carly pulled on a scarf, heavy like a towel. It reminded him of the other scarf with the gold thread back at his flat. Carly's scarf looked like a turban. Her hair was damp, eyes sullen, pointed face.

'How long are you here?' she asked, reaching over to a brush.

He sensed her animosity and glanced around the room, not wanting the arguments to begin again, people blaming him. Dan leant back against the wall.

'I don't know, it depends on Tess. I saw her this morning.'

'Yeah? What did she say?'

'Nothing much, she talked about Benjy. A guy came to see her. His name's Brandt.'

He wondered where the statue was that he'd taken from Benjy's place. Dan left the room and he followed him down to his bedroom.

He sat down and leant back against a pillow, glancing over to a chest of drawers, wondering if it was there. He'd given it to Dan before he went to jail.

'People are saying Tess has a kid,' Dan said. 'She's been in the city with her mother. She hasn't been back long from overseas. Have you asked her about it?'

He remembered the kid back at Emilia's. He'd sensed Tess had lost her nerve when he was there at the house, that she wanted to tell him something but couldn't.

'No, I thought she wanted to say something today but she backed down. You know she didn't want to see me. Maybe the kid's someone else's.'

'I think she was pregnant when you went to jail. She went overseas and had him over there, cut off contact with everyone. I reckon he's yours. He looks like you. You were in jail and she went overseas not long after.'

He remembered the dark man he'd seen at the pub and at Roland's, how they looked similar. 'People told me she had a fling with a guy who looked like me. Maybe it's him. I saw a guy today, watching me. He looked like me.'

'Javier. He's a friend of hers. He works as a chef at the resort. She knew him overseas but she was pregnant before she left. The kid's yours, I'm sure.'

'Emilia didn't say anything but I guess she thought it was up to Tess to tell me.'

'Yeah, I guess so,' said Dan.

He picked up a glass from the table, looking at the residue inside and wondered if Tess knew what had happened with Benjy. Maybe this Javier saw him as a threat, the way he was staring at him, watching him all the time. He leant back on the bed, trying to assess what Dan was thinking.

'Emilia and Tess were pretty tight for a time, but then things got worse between them, all the arguments about Benjy and Ruby, that girl he was supposed to have abused. I could tell she was affected by it and then today Emilia said Tess was in a bad way as if she was using again.'

'Yeah, Tess distanced herself from Emilia. Did you say anything to Tess about Dad?' He frowned when he mentioned his stepfather.

'No, nothing. So the kid's been with her mother while she's been settling in here?'

'Yeah.'

He could hear the tone in Dan's voice, conscious that Emilia and Tess were still at odds with each other. They'd been estranged for a time. Emilia was protective of her as her younger sister but there was contempt in her tone as if she were wasting her time. He already knew Tess had had a relationship with another man just before he'd left. Maybe it was this Javier. The child could be his. How would Dan know anyway?

'There's something about Angela. What do you think of her? She knows Benjy.' He sensed Dan's interest pick up.

'Yeah, I know what you mean. Someone told me Brandt, that guy she knows, worked for Benjy's family. He was close friends with Benjy's brother.'

'I heard they want to clear his name.'

'I think that's just a front. Tess doesn't think it was real.'

'Funny, she was definite about it when I first heard. Why would Ruby's mother make it up?'

'I don't know. Xanthe messed people around. I think she overreacted. That's what Tess said.'

He flinched when Dan said this and glanced around the room. He sensed Dan's reticence but they had a code between them.

'Benjy had that thing about South America. Someone said they saw him there. He met someone over there. Everyone knew he was having some kind of problem. The cops looked into it but decided he was overseas. He aggravated people in the city, stepped on people's toes. The cops don't care. I never got involved in it. Benjy was moving in on other people's territory.'

He sensed Dan pulling back. It made him uneasy again when he thought about it all. The furnishings were cheap, an iron bed with a chenille bedspread, a dirty Venetian blind. He knew Dan didn't believe him.

'Does Angela see Lyle?'

'I haven't been up at Tanglewood for a while myself. I'm not sure. Paul said there's a new road there but they still haven't cleared that path. I heard Paul got into a fight with someone there. I never liked going there, the potholes, and then it was so far away, all the bush.'

He felt irritated by Dan and watched him packing things away. The darkness came into his mind again. There was a feeling of not belonging. Dan was drifting away. He studied him, feeling anxious and wondered if he knew what he'd done, if he could trust him. He'd overreacted when Benjy refused to pay him the money he owed but there was more to it, his anger about the girl's abuse. Glancing over at a surfboard in the corner, he was conscious of Dan's distance, and remembered making love with Tess at Tanglewood, the shadows on the wall, the warmth of her body.

'We should find out what happened to our mother,' he said, trying to distract himself.

He could hear the flatness in his voice and Dan stared back at him.

'Yeah, I guess so.' Dan's voice was mechanical. It was as if he were trying to say the right thing to please him, but didn't really believe it.

He could tell Dan was afraid of him and thought of the child at Emilia's, knowing that Tess blamed him, thought he wasn't fit to be the kid's father. That's why she was being evasive and would probably say he was someone else's kid, even if he wasn't.

'What's the boy's name?' he asked. 'Tess's kid.'

'Benedict after her grandfather.'

'Benedict?'

'Yeah, after her grandfather. He's called Ben.'

Ben was like Benjy. He didn't like this.

'Benedict's like Benjy,' he said, thinking aloud.

'He's not Benjy's kid.'

'How do you know?'

'I can tell. He's yours, just the way he looks.' Dan said nothing more.

He'd heard of people thinking they were the fathers of kids out of wishful thinking and then the kid turned out to be someone else's. Tess's grandfather came into his mind. He was a clever man by all accounts, kind too. He remembered now his name was Benedict. Then he re-membered the child at Emilia's, how he'd seemed unpleasant, but if he was being fair, it was more that he seemed a little restless, not really the disturbing or ghostly image he'd seen through the doorway. Yes, he was being unfair. It all seemed different now. There was a point when he'd moved closer and noticed the dark circles beneath his eyes. Not many people knew what had happened to him with his stepfather. He stared at Dan, wondering why he never said anything at the time, fear and shame, disgust and disbelief. Maybe the kid at Emilia's was Benjy's. Benjy had that pale look. He was confused about it all.

Dan walked back towards the living room and he followed him to the spare room, feeling tense.

'Do you think the kid could be Benjy's?'

Dan turned to look at him. 'No.'

This didn't reassure him. He could hear scratching somewhere.

Clothes and papers overflowed from suitcases onto the carpet and around the spare room. Dan tried to clear some of it away.

'Who's staying here?'

'No one. It's my shit.'

'Are you going away?'

'Just clearing things up. I want to do some repairs.'

He cast a disapproving eye around the debris, thinking that he couldn't stay at Dan's. Dan couldn't even offer accommodation. His messiness disgusted him. He remembered how he'd tried sleeping here once but there were scratchings behind the wall, the scampering and running of animals. He imagined them running across his body and face.

'What are you going to do?'

He shrugged, imagining the clawing of animals at his skin. 'I'll see what Tess wants. I want to know what's happening with my kid, why she didn't tell me.'

Dan rummaged in a drawer and pulled out the statue. 'Here, take it. I don't want it any more. It's bad luck.' He thrust it at him.

It was the sculpture of a panther he'd taken from Benjy's place, powerful limbs, mouth with fanged teeth. It was a kind of caricature in a way but beautiful. It seemed to stare at him savagely, mocking him. The sleek lines of its body and eyes were alluring. It was the sort of thing that Roland would like, quirky and beautiful at the same time. He studied the eyes. Did panthers have green eyes? He didn't know. Like everything else, something about it was illusory.

'It's classy, isn't it?'

Dan nodded uninterestedly.

'Why don't you like it?'

'I get a bad feeling about it.'

'Don't be stupid. I wonder where he got it. Benjy didn't have any money. Why would he have something like this?'

'An heirloom. I heard Tess talking about it.'

'An heirloom? You're kidding!'

'Tess told me it belonged to someone he knew, someone his grand-father knew, a friend of his, something to do with World War II. They're looking for it, the family. I wouldn't sell it. I mean, I don't trust Lyle or any of his friends, and neither should you. Don't do it through him.'

'So that's why they want to find out what happened to Benjy. It's the statue. I'm not doing it through Lyle. I mightn't be here much longer. You're right. I'll see someone else about it.'

'Be careful of Lyle, Mick. I don't like what's happening. He's up to something.'

He glanced down the hallway, wondering if it was really about the statue. The door was open. Carly was talking to someone on the landing. The light flicked back as she walked out through the door. She pressed it. It flicked on again and a thin skeletal man glanced at him, completely emotionless, dead eyes. He stared back at him in the dim stairwell, his eyes unseeing.

'Mick, be careful of Lyle.'

He turned back, distracted. 'Yeah, okay. I'm not scared of him.' He pulled away, bothered by Dan's comments. What if Benjy's son, Seth, had seen something and had been talking to Lyle?

He sat down on a chair, wondering what Lyle was up to, as Dan cleared things away, packing.

Dan pulled himself up from the suitcase.

Tess had seemed edgy today. Maybe Lyle had threatened her. He remembered the bougainvillea in the church, the woman who'd stared at him as he walked out. He felt something dark twist inside him as he stared up at the wall.

'Tess hasn't been back here long, Mick. I thought she was involved with Joss Cameron, but I think the kid's yours. She and Joss are friends. Carly doesn't think she was involved with him or Javier either.'

He got up from the chair, and gazed out the window, recalling all the rumours.

'I don't think she's with Joss any more, Mick,' said Dan. He was standing by the doorway. 'She was only with him for a while after you went to jail. He visited her overseas. I don't know about Javier. He's protective of her for some reason.'

He noticed Dan staring down at the floor. Something about him was troubling him, and again he wondered if he could trust him. He remembered how his mother refused to do anything about his stepfather and wondered what had happened to her. He walked around a table, thinking about his mother, and remembered the fake jewels on Yasmin's dress, how they gleamed, but were only glass. He felt his hands clench, thinking of the jewels in the panther's eyes. Were they real? It was on the table and he studied it, the glint in the light. The beads in his mother's necklace came into his mind, how Roxanne, his stepfather's lover, had been wearing them, how they all gleamed but were only glass.

'Tess never told me about my son. I never knew about him,' he said bitterly. His hands tensed again and he clenched them, staring at Dan. 'I'm taking a while to get used to it. It's difficult settling back, the wide spaces bother me. Does that make sense? I was supposed to see Lyle at the pub but he didn't show up. He was supposed to find me work. I guess I'll have to find my own work.'

'I told you not to trust him. I heard they're looking for experienced builders at Dolphin Point. They're building that huge place. Suzanne told me. I think you'll be okay, Mick. Lyle was always jealous of you. He's the one stirring it up. People see through him.'

He glanced over towards the door, grateful Dan was reassuring him, but knowing it could all be false. Dan was similar to their mother, dark and slim, something about him reminded him of her and he felt melancholy.

He turned away from Dan, feeling uneasy, wondering what he was going to do about everything. His mind focused on the boy. He knew he wasn't fit to be a father, that's why Tess hadn't told him. He suspected she wasn't really involved with Joss or Javier and was in denial about the kid's paternity. Emilia had said she thought Tess was still using but she seemed distracted about other things. He remembered the beginnings of a track near Emilia's place. It led down to the bay and further into the hinterland. It was called Tanglewood Path and it veered off and continued on until you reached a remote beach further north. Tess found the track and the beach too isolated, unsettling in spite of their beauty. He'd taken her there once, and she'd seemed unnerved by it. Tanglewood was further along the road where Paul and Suzanne lived.

'Paul mentioned the statue,' said Dan suddenly. 'It was while you were away. They were all talking about it. Angela said it sounded beautiful.' He frowned when he mentioned Angela.

'It is beautiful. That's one reason Brandt's here. I'm sure of it. It's valuable.'

Dan smiled slightly.

He remembered his stepfather again, wrestling with him, and then the kid at Emilia's, something strange about him. 'Forget it,' he said, trying to cover his tracks and appear more focused. 'Maybe Benjy wasn't really as bad as people thought. He did some dealing and he was a womaniser but he had an okay side. At least that's what Yasmin thinks.'

Dan raised his eyebrows.

'Tess said he was misunderstood. I wondered if there was something to it. Tess was suspicious of him, then she changed. She said Xanthe, Ruby's mother, had a grievance against him.'

'Yeah, that's how she came across to me too at first, Tess, I mean, but I think it was true.'

'So you think it was real?'

'Yeah, of course.'

He smiled at Dan uncomfortably and left the room, walking down the hall into the kitchen, thinking about Tess. He noticed a car below through the window. A man climbed out. It was Roland's friend Justin, the guy he'd seen walking past him in the street when he'd left Roland's. He watched him walk to the door purposefully, wondering what was happening. He walked back out and sat down on a couch.

Dan had suggested once that Emilia wasn't as confident and resilient as she appeared to be, that she could distort the facts sometimes. It was she who had talked to him about Ruby's abuse. Emilia didn't like to admit her own failings to herself because it frightened her, her vulnerability. Obviously her husband, John, who was a lawyer, could turn on the charm, but why would someone as intelligent and independent as Emilia keep going when he was dragging her down. Something to do with her and Tess's parents, he guessed, unresolved issues. She never spoke about them. Tess, on the other hand, had spoken a lot about their parents. She'd already commented that Emilia and John were emotionally dependent on one another, but John was the sort of person who ground you down emotionally. Tess had detached from it all. In the past, Emilia wouldn't have anything bad said about him because she didn't want to admit she'd made a mistake. It was self-indulgent, she said, and she had too many things on her mind.

He remembered the nightclub where he'd met Tess. Emilia was part owner of it. Tess had been standing under the light and looked strangely old-fashioned. Her auburn hair swept past her shoulders, the intricate strands of her silver shawl fragile like the threads of a spider's web. She was different to the type of women he went out with. Her dark skirt revealed the pale curve of her legs, slender in the clarity of the light. He'd seen her from a distance and someone told him she was Emilia's sister. He'd worked with Emilia at the resort. People had been surprised at the way he'd been friends with her, assuming that someone from his background would never be of interest to her, but Emilia and Tess weren't entirely as they appeared. He guessed he'd proven them right in the end.

The doorbell rang and Dan got up to answer it. It was Justin, the guy he'd passed on the road after he'd left Roland's. He wondered if he'd been sent as some kind of emissary for Roland or Lyle. He remembered seeing Benjy from behind. Only the back of his head was visible, and an intense disgust had taken hold.

Justin walked in and sat down on the couch. He leant back, glancing about the room.

Dan frowned from the corner as if warning him.

He realised Justin had been privy to discussions about what was going on, the armed robbery, his deteriorating state of mind before he went to jail, his drinking. People had said he was losing it. He wondered if he'd imagined it all, the situation with Benjy and Ruby, but something had happened with her. He was sure of it. Was there someone else who could have done it? Tess had said Xanthe had a grievance against Benjy.

Emilia was certain it was Benjy but then maybe she was wrong. He wondered who the people were who Benjy was supposed to have helped, the reason Yasmin had said he was kind.

'How was jail, Callaghan?' said Justin.

'I'm different, you know,' he said, trying to sound confident. 'I thought about things inside. I don't really want to get involved in any of it any more.'

Justin looked at him sceptically. 'Yeah, Tess said that.'

The door was ajar and he could hear someone walking downstairs.

'Tess always said you were smart. I can understand why you'd want to start a new life. Nobody expected you to get into such a mess. Tess said it was all to do with other stuff.'

He didn't want to hear any of this.

'Everyone knows you're smart. Don't look at me like that. Why would you get dragged into it all?'

He could tell Justin was fishing for information. He wondered if he knew what was going on, if this was a dig at Dan, who had dragged him into the robbery because he'd wanted money too, if he was interested in the statue.

'I did all right at the resort. Emilia gave me a chance and I disappointed her. Maybe I can get back to it. I saw her today. She seemed okay. Anyway, I don't know what's been happening.'

Justin studied him and he sensed he was hiding things. He wondered if he knew about the murder. His mind drifted to Tess again. He was conscious of the antagonism in Justin's voice, and then his reserve, as if he were backing away from him.

His eyes drifted to his hands. Maybe Benjy hadn't been involved in anything. He watched Justin pick up the lighter on the table and begin playing with it.

He thought of Seth, Benjy's kid. He was a strange kid, given to telling stories and had been aggressive from a young age. He'd never liked him. He remembered an incident when Seth told him he was an arsehole. He was right of course but he didn't take that sort of backchat from a kid.

'Do you know Angela's friend, Brandt? Tess mentioned him today. He was asking about Benjy.'

Justin had a serious expression on his face. 'Yeah, they're worried about Suzanne. They knew you used to be close to Benjy. Seth's a basket case.'

He pulled back when Justin said this and thought of Angela, her pale skin, and the tumble of dark curls around her face, a reddish tint to her hair. She'd mentioned seeing Suzanne and Paul. The pink stone he'd seen at the marina came into his mind again.

'I should get away,' he said tensely. 'Start a new life with Tess.'

Justin's serious look reminded him of the woman in the church and that image of barbed wire returned, the dark figure of a man looking down, watching him. He remembered the dark guy who looked like him at the pub, Javier, the guy Tess knew. That unpleasant sense of foreboding returned that something was shadowing him. As he looked across the room, he knew he was being watched.

'I feel bad for Seth,' he lied.

'Yeah, we all do. Tess said her kid plays with Seth, that Seth looks after him.'

He shifted slightly; troubled that his kid was involved with the kid of the man he'd killed. 'Really? How old is Seth now, sixteen?'

'Yeah, he looks after him, that's what I meant. Angela seems to have a low opinion of him.'

'Seth?'

'Yeah, she doesn't like him.'

'You knew Benjy when you were in the city, didn't you? I didn't like the way he treated Suzanne.'

'Yeah, but he could be okay.'

Laughter drifted from outside across the garden. He could hear Carly's voice. When he glanced up, Dan had left the room.

'So you knew Benjy well in the city?'

'Yeah, I knew them all but I didn't know you knew them too. Paul's worried about Seth.'

'Paul only cares about himself. Suzanne has some money. Maybe he's after her money. Seth's a strange kid. I think they're covering up about something.'

He didn't think Seth had seen anything, or at least not him. It was probably Lyle he'd seen at the house. The police had been suspicious of him, had focused all their attention on him. He knew Seth didn't like him. He didn't like Lyle either. Lyle had dark hair, was tall and thin, similar to himself. He glanced at Justin, thinking he was tall and dark too, and so was Javier, so it could be any of them, but Javier was a heavier build, like a guy he'd known in jail. He remembered the entrance at Benjy's again, the burnt, charred smell of meat wafting towards him in the air from a barbecue. He'd found the statue of the panther there after he'd killed him. Seth could have gone down there himself. Maybe he'd seen the statue earlier, taken whatever was inside it. There was a cavity in it but there was nothing there when he found it.

Justin looked contemplative. 'How long are you here, Mick?'

'It depends.'

'On what?'

He shrugged. 'Tess.'

'You know Tess wasn't expecting you to come back.'

He felt uneasy now, all these people looking out for Tess.

'There were bad memories of course. I'm surprised she came back herself. She seemed determined to come back for some reason.'

He stared at Justin, knowing he was taunting him. 'Apparently Dan thinks her kid's mine.'

He remembered the darkness of the trees next to the rocks, similar to the trees near Tess's, and the ocean. He felt paranoid again, thinking of the waves lashing the rocks, rising up.

Justin studied him. He seemed distant now, but when he glanced back, he smiled sympathetically. 'Yeah, I heard about the kid. You should be careful, Mick. There are people around here who knew Benjy. They're wondering about other people who knew him. I don't know if they're connected with Brandt.'

'Who is this Brandt?'

Justin glanced away from him. 'Brandt's a friend of Benjy's brother. Benjy owed a lot of people money, including Lyle. A lot of people hated him. Emilia was angry about the girl he was supposed to have abused. Paul hated him because of Suzanne. The list goes on and on.'

He studied the balcony and leaves on the trees. Justin smiled at him, slightly. He could feel himself losing it and remembered the man down the hallway. Angela had said he was a friend. He turned quickly, glancing back towards Justin.

Justin's voice had an angry tone and he bit his lip. Feeling uncomfortable, he glanced back again. The cops had questioned him briefly about the money Benjy owed him but decided it was nothing. It was only a small amount and there were others who were owed much larger amounts. He studied the window and wondered if this was why Angela had been so suspicious of him. She probably knew about the statue too.

Justin was staring at him now in that odd, intense way that he'd become accustomed to.

He could hear Dan downstairs with Carly. He bit his lip slightly and thought of Angela, her slim build and fine features. The overall effect was marred by her thin lips, a feature he didn't like in a woman.

He remembered the statue. He wasn't sure if the eyes were jewels, the trimmings were silver. It had ivory fangs.

Justin pulled back as if he were wary of him.

He could tell it had taken some effort coming over here. There was something confusing about it all, just as there had been with Tess when they were together back at the house. They were all suspicious of him, he realised, and it was making him paranoid. He glanced around, remembering his stepfather.

'I know it's bad what happened. We were both in a bad way, Tess and I, but we're both different now.' He sounded trite and knew it.

Justin frowned at him. 'Like I said, Mick, there are people around here who knew Benjy. They're wondering about other people who knew him.'

He looked away from him, knowing Justin was warning him.

Justin said nothing further, and he remembered Benjy had seemed overly interested in Ruby, like he was grooming her. It was like his own abuse. He was sure he'd done it. But maybe Benjy was just being solicitous. He hadn't cared about it when that friend of Xanthe's had approached him. He'd told him to fuck off, but there was something strange about it all.

'I'm on edge all the time,' he said, backing down and feeling nervous. 'You get suspicious of everyone. I think Tess and I should go away. She didn't tell me she was involved with anyone.'

'You're right. I heard you had a bad time inside.'

He sat back, wondering if Justin was trying to unnerve him. 'Not really, there was a guy there who had it in for me but I didn't let it get to me. I'm tougher than I look.'

To his surprise, Justin said, 'You care about people, Mick. I mean about Tess and other things. You can't deal with it all.'

He studied him, annoyed. Justin was trying to get into his head. It seemed odd that he was analysing him this way, and he was suspicious of him again.

'You know, the police think Lyle killed him.'

Justin nodded and he studied him curiously. 'Maybe. I heard something about that.'

He was conscious of the antagonism in his voice. His eyes drifted to Justin's hands, a wedding ring. Who was he married to?

Justin pulled a lighter from his pocket and began playing with it, twisting it back and forth. Then he smiled at him cunningly, his pale face, and his finger adorned with the wedding ring. He was staring at him and he felt a subtle pressure coming from him as if he wanted something, but it was difficult to fathom what it was, and why he was playing around with him. He appeared to be hesitating as if he were contemplating his next move, playing a cat and mouse game. As he shifted in his seat, he knew again that he was being watched.

Images flooded his memory of Benjy's body flailing in the water. He remembered the ghostly image contorting desperately, something brushing his arms, a leaf, creepy. The touch of it made him flinch, like dead skin, Benjy's scream, the coldness of a lifeless body.

He felt his head pounding, remembering the waves rising up like a hissing demon from the sand and then the child through the doorway at Emilia's. The child was doomed like himself.

'There was a kid at Emilia's. Dan thinks he's my kid. He looked really unhappy to me.' He felt troubled thinking about the child.

Justin frowned at him. 'Yeah, I don't know. He has asthma, something like that.'

'Asthma? I had that as a kid.'

'Yeah, I think it's that,' said Justin. 'Look, I'd better go.' He seemed unsettled now and stood up, walking to the door.

'I'll see you later,' he called out to him.

Justin nodded and walked downstairs.

He sat there for a while, thinking about it all.

'What did he want?' asked Dan, walking into the living room.

'Nothing,' he said.

Dan studied him suspiciously. 'What's the matter?'

'Nothing,' he repeated. 'He was just trying to get into my head, although he warned me like you. Look, I have to go. I have things to do.' He stood up stiffly and walked into the spare room to get the statue. Then he returned to the living room.

'What are you going to do?' asked Dan.

'I'm going to see Tess.'

Dan nodded at him and he walked downstairs to the car, remembering how he'd bent down near the pool at Roland's towards a leaf, the poinsettia petals blood-red in the moonlight. He was distracted as he walked along the road, noticing lights hovering indistinctly in the distance. He could see the lights now and climbed into the car, wondering where they were. Turning on the ignition and starting the car, he followed the road, feeling troubled by the memories, firstly of his stepfather, and then Benjy, the way his stepfather had grabbed his arm and he'd wrenched himself free, struggled with him.

A steeply wooded hillside rose on the right. Fir trees lined the beach, pools ringed with rocks. He remembered that fragile leaf the night he'd killed Benjy. It fluttered onto his hand and he'd felt that chilling sense of shifting, like he was nothing really, just something vague and ghostly in the car. He'd studied the intricate lines like a spidery skeleton, something that had drifted down onto his lap. He'd flicked it away aggressively. It was a phantom leaf, imaginary, a silvery ghost that he would never let get into his head.

Towards the end of the road near the park, he noticed the light flickering, the same light he'd seen earlier. He remembered that splatter of blood, a short cry in the night, Benjy edging away from him.

Driving back along the highway, an unpleasant memory returned of a string of glass beads, and a woman pouring black liquid over her hair. She was naked from the waist up. He'd seen her through the doorway. He remembered his stepfather and other men having sex with her. She was towelling herself dry, running the towel over her body. The water on her skin glistened brightly in the sun.

Panic gripped him as he thought of Benjy struggling, the way he'd held his arm out, and an image flashed through his mind of a man's body, and then a pile of ashes which were scattered by the wind and blown away into the night's obscurity.

When he arrived back, he saw Angela on her balcony. She turned quickly and walked back inside. He strolled towards the building, bothered by memories of his stepfather.

Climbing the stairs to his flat, he unlocked the door and walked out to the balcony. He could hear people down below. When he glanced down, Angela was talking to someone. Leaning forward, he noticed some of her bougainvillea in a vase on the table. He reached over towards it, and a tiny beetle crawled out from his shirt and made its way along his arm. He flicked it away aggressively.

Feeling irritated by the beetle, he walked back inside and sat down. Leaning back on the couch, he wondered what he was going to do about Tess and the kid. There was a knock at the door and he got up to answer it. Angela was standing there with the man he'd seen in the hallway before he'd driven with her into town.

'Mick, this is Brandt.'

Brandt's face was heavily tanned and scored by the sun. He felt strangely intimidated by his robust appearance and the mocking directness of his gaze.

'Tess told me she saw you today,' he said, watching Brandt's reaction.

'Yeah, I know her mother.'

He shifted slightly, surprised that Brandt knew Tess's mother. He remembered Tess had been staying with her mother in the city.

He motioned them inside. There was an unpleasantness in Brandt's tone that made him uneasy. He sat down opposite and Angela followed him in. He remembered being frightened of his stepfather, how he'd been pleasant at first then he'd started to turn. He had the same dominating presence as Brandt.

A large ceiling fan whirled overhead, creating tiny eddies of wind. A line of palms, tall and statuesque, led from his stepfather's house to the road and beyond the palms, a series of cliffs, black and streaked with green, towered like sentinels above the ocean. The sharp angle of the road swept down towards the bay, flanked by dense green forest and the irregular hump of the headland. His stepfather's house had been on the hill.

'What do you want?' he asked, trying to block out the memories. 'How do you know Tess's mother?'

'Just people we both know. Tess's mother said your stepfather was a businessman but your real father was a traveller, a gypsy or something.'

'Yeah, my father abandoned my brother and me when we were young. So did my mother. My stepfather raised us.'

He rummaged in his pocket and felt the ten-dollar note he'd found on the ground earlier. He pulled it out and studied it. When he looked up, he noticed the sharp lines of Angela's face. Her wide mouth was smeared with lipstick, pale blue eyes. He wondered if they were trying to draw him into a discussion about his stepfather. Then he remembered Roxanne, his stepfather's younger lover. She knew Benjy, that's how he'd met him.

Angela looked angry as if she'd had enough of him.

'I heard you knew Benjy's brother,' he said to Brandt, trying to stall a bit.

'Yeah, Benjy didn't do anything to that girl. You know – Ruby, I mean the one who was supposed to have been abused. I think his disappearance is connected, though.'

Standing up, he walked out to the balcony, feeling nervous. Yasmin was on the other side of the garden down below. He could see her with the guy she was with at Roland's, the one she was dancing with. He felt annoyed, watching her. The man looked young, too young for her, and was scruffily dressed.

'What do you think of Clinton?' he asked, walking back inside.

Angela sighed and looked away. 'He treated Yasmin badly. She's very fragile.' She was standing by the doorway, dressed in a black satin dress shirred around the breasts. Her eyebrows were arched, her hair dark, skin, creamy like alabaster.

He reached for a cigarette and began fiddling with it.

Brandt glanced back towards the balcony. 'People said Benjy had a stash out there.'

'Money?'

'Yeah.'

Justin had warned him about people knowing Benjy who were interested in other people who knew him. He flicked some ash out into a bowl. Angela moved back inside.

He couldn't resist playing with them. It was risky, commenting on the money, but it was amusing. Anyway, the police already suspected there was money there.

'Really, he had some money out there?'

'Yeah, Seth's a mess really,' said Angela. 'He's starting to remember things.'

'I feel bad for Seth,' he lied. 'Benjy wasn't a good father. He was an arsehole. Seth's better off without him.'

'Seth's very disturbed,' said Angela.

He glanced up at her. She had a strained expression on her face.

'Yeah, Justin said he was a mess.'

'People can be good and bad,' said Angela, watching him. 'It's not straightforward.'

'Good and bad? What does that mean?' He was conscious that Angela was staring at him, a slight smirk on her lips. He sensed Brandt watching him too. His mind drifted to Tess again, thinking about his son. He'd been conscious of the antagonism in her voice. He watched Brandt pick up the lighter on the table and begin playing with it.

'You look worried, Mick.' Brandt's tone was mocking. He was smiling at him now and he looked across the room at Angela.

'Look, it's late,' he said. 'I don't want to talk about this any more. Leave me alone.'

'Yeah, okay, Mick,' said Angela. 'We're going.' She stood up and walked to the door, looking annoyed.

Brandt stood by the doorway. He was staring at him and he sat there waiting for them to leave. Brandt closed the door behind him.

He was overreacting, he knew it, but he didn't like Brandt's tone. He could tell by their reactions that they thought he was guilty of something. Images flooded his memory of his stepfather and then Benjy. He'd managed to block it out. Then he remembered that ghostly image contorting desperately, something brushing his arms. It was after he'd killed Benjy. Brandt didn't really know what had happened.

He felt his head pounding, thinking of the rocks, the blue lights on the ocean, the darkness of the waves as he'd cruised out to the ocean the next day. He turned quickly, glancing back at a pattern on the wall, a fading shadow of gold.

He could hear them both outside in the corridor, laughing, and he walked into the bedroom. Staring up at the wall, he remembered walking towards the car, noticing someone in the distance. He'd been distracted watching them.

The black scarf caught his eye and he thought of Benjy. It was too bad what had happened. He couldn't take any chances.

Studying the statue now on the bed, he picked it up, noticing the gleam of its eyes. There was a poster of a bird on the wall. Tess had said once, 'Birds are a symbol of the soul and the infinite.'

There was no infinite for him. He lay down on the bed, feeling exhausted. Darkness closed in and he could feel himself slipping, drifting off to sleep.

*

The next morning, his head was aching. The ten-dollar bill was still in his pocket. He pulled it out and stared at it, then he noticed the statue on a chair near the bed. He picked it up, staring at the eyes.

He got dressed and decided to go into town before he saw Tess. Glancing back as he left the building, he noticed Angela's balcony. It was empty. The bougainvillea had gone. There was that sensation again that he was being watched. Feeling anxious, he climbed into the car, and drove through town, wondering where Angela had gone.

Pulling over, he rang Tess. 'I have to see you. I think you know what it's about.'

'Okay,' she replied abruptly. 'Come in half an hour.'

The Blue Toucan Café was up ahead, a large figure of a blue bird with a dark eye staring down at the street. He put the phone away and walked towards the café. As he walked inside, he stared at his reflection in the mirrors on the wall, dark skin, wavy black hair, eyes that were almost black. A woman was behind the counter, wearing a demure black skirt, close around the hips and a patterned blouse. She looked like a waitress from the movies he used to watch as a kid. A couple of men in the corner were watching him.

He ordered a coffee, drinking it slowly, listening to a conversation about tourists and fishing expeditions. He paid the waitress and left the café, walking down the street, then he remembered the whale. It had swum down the river from the sea and had lost its way. It had been there for months and he couldn't remember what had happened to it.

Flicking back plastic strips, he walked inside the fish shop. A man was at the counter, short and bloated with grey hair and a florid face, dressed in a white apron. He dipped fish in batter, and fried chips, salting them with a large silver salt shaker.

A ring of sweat gathered around the neck of his top and around his thighs. Buying some cigarettes and ginger beer, he walked back to the car. A cloud of flies circled around him as he opened the door. Climbing in, he began driving towards Tess's, feeling nervous.

Passing by the turn-off to the rock platform, he continued until he reached the road through the bush that led to Tess's place. Parking the car, he walked to the door.

After a few moments, he rang the bell. Tess opened the door and motioned him inside. They walked out to the back and she stared at him nervously as she sat down. He could hear noises from outside that sounded like a child.

'I've been hearing about a kid. Dan says he's mine.' He sat there, staring at her defiantly.

She flinched away from him and immediately he felt suspicious, knowing that she hadn't wanted him to come back. He knew she'd wanted nothing to do with him.

'Emilia didn't say anything but I guess she thought it was up to you to tell me.'

Her whole body was tense. 'Yeah, you're right. She's disappointed in me, I guess. I've been trying to rebuild the relationship.'

He noticed her flinch again and she bent over, picking up a glass from the table, gripping the stem. He leant back on the couch, trying to assess what she was thinking, if she and Emilia were becoming close again. They'd been pretty inseparable for a time, keeping people at bay, but he remembered Emilia had said Tess was using again.

'I wanted nothing to do with you, Mick. You know that.'

'Are you using?'

'No,' she said angrily. 'I distanced myself from everyone. Ben's been with a friend while I've been settling in here. Emilia and I were estranged.'

He could hear the anger in her voice and wondered if she was lying about it all, why she'd come back. Perhaps it was to repair her relationship with Emilia. They'd been close for a long time. The child mightn't be his but then why would she lie? Her dark eyes narrowed and she gazed back at him moodily now. He remembered the boy at Emilia's the day before. He'd only been here three weeks and didn't know what was happening.

She rearranged herself on her chair, still looking tense. 'Ben's been with a friend in the city,' she repeated. 'I've only been here a short while. I haven't discussed it with people.' The words seemed to tumble out.

She'd fallen out with a lot of people before she left and hadn't been here long herself. He knew she didn't trust people. No doubt, she didn't want anyone questioning her about what she'd been doing overseas, and he didn't know what she'd been doing himself. He wondered if the child was really his. He felt his neck tense. Perhaps she'd decided it was better to be involved with someone who could provide a future for the kid.

'So his name's Ben?' he said sourly. 'Similar to Benjy, isn't it?' He studied her, suspiciously.

'It's my grandfather's name,' she said quickly.

Her maternal expression irritated him. It didn't suit her. Something didn't seem right.

'How old is he?'

'Five.'

The kid had a pale complexion. Tess's complexion was pale, so was Benjy's. His own skin was swarthy. People said he had an exotic look and women found him attractive, that's as long as he kept his worst side hidden. Tess's type was dark hair, slim build, like himself. Benjy didn't look like that. All of his instincts were on a setting of distrust. The kid did look like him, though, the lean face and high cheekbones, the expression, a little defiant and detached, mocking almost, and then the eyes, steady, as if penetrating your thoughts. Someone had said that about him once, that he looked right through people. Perhaps Tess had started to suspect what he was thinking as she pulled back, looking annoyed.

'It was my grandfather's name. You remember my grandfather.'

'Yeah, I remember. He was smart, wasn't he?'

'Yeah, he was an engineer.'

This was the sort of thing he didn't like about Tess, how she made him feel inferior because she'd had a better education, a better background. She'd been attracted to him because he was different, and she hated her family. He stared at her, thinking that the name Benedict sounded like Benjy. It made him uneasy. Had she had more of a connection with Benjy than he knew?

'But when did you know you were pregnant?' He was unable to keep the angry tone from his voice. 'Was it around the time I went to jail?'

'Yeah, it was then.' She leant back on the couch with an odd satisfied look. 'You remember we split up. I didn't want to have anything to do with you.'

He sat there, processing it all, suspicious about the boy. He wondered if she had any intention of allowing him to see him. It was obvious she'd only told him to stop speculation and might even prefer to think the boy's father was someone else.

'I'd like to meet him,' he said, flatly. 'My son, I mean.'

'Yeah, of course.'

She seemed evasive now but he was intrigued about the child, in spite of being repelled, an odd mixture of panic and elation. There was a detachment in her tone that made him uneasy. He felt suspicious and wondered if she was testing him, or worse, lying.

'Why didn't you go to Roland's?'

'I was busy,' she said. 'He's still the same, you know. I don't hang out with that crowd any more.'

Roland had always been a source of amusement to her, his swimming pool that was the size of a small lake.

'I thought you liked him?'

'Yeah, I do, but I don't see him much.'

'I might have a look at Tanglewood,' he said. 'I heard Benjy's son's with Paul and Suzanne, that he's causing problems. I'm surprised Suzanne took up with Paul. She didn't like him at the beginning.'

'Yeah, Ben and Seth like each other in spite of the age difference. The guy who was looking for you, he knows Angela and my mother.'

He felt uncomfortable again thinking that his kid was associating with the child of the man he'd killed, and then that his suspicions about Angela were right, that she was more involved with them than she let on.

'How does he know your mother?'

'He did some building work for a friend of hers. Seth saw something the day Benjy disappeared. Did I tell you about that?'

'Yeah, you did.' He glanced away towards the window, feeling nervous.

'Someone at the house, a man. He was in the distance and he couldn't tell who it was.'

'Why didn't he mention it at the time?'

'Traumatised, I guess.'

'People have false memories, especially kids.'

She picked up her glass again. 'I guess so. I don't know. He seemed definite about it.'

'It was probably Lyle,' he said, watching her tilt the glass. 'He worked with Benjy. I heard the police questioned him. I was supposed to see him yesterday. He was going to get me some building work at the Ferguson's. They're building a house out at Dolphin Point. Dan told me. I heard Seth was causing a lot of problems at school. He was always a messed up kid.'

'I don't think he was that bad. You can be critical, Mick.'

He stared back at her, conscious that she was annoyed at him. His eyes narrowed, remembering how there had been animosity between them before they broke up. He wondered again if she was testing him.

'I hadn't seen Benjy for ages. I don't understand why you didn't tell me about the kid.'

'I'm sorry I didn't tell you. You were in jail, that's why I didn't tell you. What do you expect? Perhaps that wasn't right, but that's the way it was.'

He realised she blamed him. Her voice was mechanical. He didn't like this at all. It didn't seem right. Tess's grandfather came into his mind, how he was clever, successful.

'I got the impression Brandt was more interested in other things.'

'I don't know. They want closure, that's what he said. They want to know what happened. He thought Benjy might have been mixed up in something, a courier or something for Lyle.'

He smiled, thinking Brandt was on the wrong track. 'Like I said, closure's overrated.' His voice was cold as he glanced around the room. He sensed her pulling back, all this rubbish about closure.

'I remember you were always scared going up to Tanglewood,' he said, watching her flinch. 'Dan never liked it either.'

He felt that agitation again. Glancing over at a piano in the corner, he remembered how there'd been a lot of anger and resentment, the way he'd left, and then jail.

She stood up and moved towards the door. She was dismissing him again, he could tell, but there was still something between them, he could sense it again, still a strange attraction, in spite of all the acrimony.

He could hear something behind him, the sound of a child's voice. When he turned, a kid was standing in the doorway. It was the kid he'd seen at Emilia's, pale skin, dark circles beneath his eyes, curly dark hair. He stared at him. His frail build made him look vulnerable. He felt drawn to him but at the same time he felt repelled.

'Ben, this is Mick.'

Ben studied him, a surly expression on his face, glancing away quickly. He wondered if he knew he was his father, and as he studied him now, he could see a resemblance, but perhaps he was imagining it. He watched as he glanced away again, unable to meet his eye. The boy's evasiveness angered him. 'I'll have to take you fishing some time,' he said, trying to sound friendly.

Ben glanced at Tess, uncertainly.

'I'll ring you tomorrow, Mick. Maybe you can take him on the weekend. I'm sorry I can't talk to you more at the moment, I'm busy, perhaps later.'

Tess moved away from him towards the boy. It was obvious she wanted to get away and probably didn't have anywhere to go at all.

'Okay,' he said. 'Ring me tomorrow.'

He left the house, conscious that she'd flinched again when he'd said 'ring me tomorrow'. He knew she was afraid of him, and then why hadn't she told him about his child? Did she suspect him of Benjy's murder? Climbing into the car, he recalled the conversation with Angela the previous day, how she thought Benjy was innocent of Ruby's abuse. Driving back through town, he wondered if Tess had been involved with him.

He pulled over at a park, noticing a young man at a tennis court, his lithe body bent back as he tossed a ball into the air. He could hear a woman scolding him half-heartedly. He was much older than Ben and he tried to imagine doing activities like this with Ben. The guy whacked the ball, the taut curve of his arm flinging the racket forcefully into the air. He watched him and noticed the dark water tower in the distance.

Following the highway back through town, he began thinking how Benjy had screamed at him that he had the wrong idea, that he wasn't guilty of anything, that he was a fool and had always overreacted.

He drove through town, feeling angry about it all. Passing along the main road, he arrived back, and stared up at the flats.

Feeling stressed, he climbed out of the car and walked inside. The door creaked open when he pushed it and he lay down on the bed, staring up at the pattern of gold flowers on the wall. It was curiously ornamental and feminine. He wondered who had lived here before him, a woman, he imagined, with refined taste, like Emilia.

Sensing Angela wasn't around, he began to feel nervous. He walked out to the balcony and looked down at Angela's balcony below. There was nothing there, no bougainvillea and no table. Walking back inside, he made lunch, frying some tomatoes and eggs, then the phone rang.

It was Tess. She sounded strangely cheerful. 'You can take Ben fishing tomorrow if you like. He wants to get to know you.'

He was surprised at the warmth in her voice and felt confused. 'Yeah, okay. Do you want to come with us?'

'I can't. I have something to do.'

He paused, wondering what was happening, if he was being given a second chance. 'When do you want me to be there?'

'Eleven,' she said.

'Okay, that's fine.' He hung up, staring at the phone, wondering what she was up to.

Breathing deeply, he stood up and walked out to the balcony. Angela's car had gone. He walked back into the flat, thinking about her visit with Brandt the night before. Lying down on the couch, he stared up at the wall. Unable to relax, he walked downstairs and down to the river. He thought he saw someone at the wharf on the island opposite.

There was a chill in the air and he walked back slowly to his flat. When he walked inside, he remembered Angela and Brandt again and he reached for the knife he'd hidden under the cushion, wondering if he should ring Lyle. He didn't trust him, though.

He slept badly that night and in the morning, he climbed out of bed, getting ready to drive to Tess's. Walking out to the balcony, he glanced down below. The table was still missing. He wondered where Angela was as he walked downstairs to the car, sensing something was happening. It was making him anxious. Climbing in, he drove along the road, not knowing what he was going to do with Ben.

The road led along the coast. Tess's place was along a back road set back towards the end. Climbing out, he walked towards the door. Tess answered the door after he rang the bell.

'Do you want to go to the beach?' he said turning to Ben, who was standing by a fish tank when they walked into the living room.

Ben shrugged and looked away from him. He studied him again. It bothered him, the angry look in his eyes.

'What are you doing?' he said to Tess, feeling a growing sense of unease.

'Something at the resort,' she said, walking towards the door. 'I'll be back later.'

Ben didn't say anything. He remembered how he played with Seth, Benjy's kid. There was that strange detachment, an unpleasant surliness in his manner.

He walked with him to the car, not saying anything himself. He had a bad flashback to his stepfather, and glanced at Ben, who was looking away from him. He could see him in profile, his high cheekbones, the thin bridge of his nose.

'We'll go further up the coast,' he said, feeling his hands tense. He could see the tension in Ben's body as if he didn't trust him.

They climbed into the car and he began driving along the coast, neither of them saying anything. He realised now that Tess was using and she'd gone to score. The long stretch of sand was visible now, like a ghost beach, and he pulled over by the side of the road. Ben moved slightly away from him.

He climbed out of the car and turned to face him. 'What's the matter?' he said coldly.

Ben stared back angrily.

Knowing he should be watching him, he walked away to the rocks, near to where he'd stood with his stepfather. He glanced up at the sandhills down the beach. His foot touched a stone and he picked it up, throwing it. It bounced onto a ledge before spinning, twisting slightly, shattering down below. He could hear the sound of rock hitting rock and was conscious of Ben watching him as he picked up another stone, smashing it harder on the rocks.

He felt the anger growing in him as he marched up to Ben and grabbed his hand. Ben pulled his hand away, and he remembered the prow of a boat, staring down at the ocean, dolphins playing in the water that splashed at the sides. He moved away from Ben and walked to the waves, plunging into the water. The tide pulled him forward, a wide strip of golden sand up ahead. Buoyed by the swell of the ocean, he moved forward effortlessly, aware of a dark shadow beneath him, undulating like the rhythmic waves of the sea. It was a manta ray and he passed by, unafraid.

Ben was in the shallows. He glanced back at him, observing his innocence as he trailed his hands in the water. He thought of Benjy struggling, calling out for help, his body drifting away, lifeless, like the fishes he left to die on the shore. He'd stabbed him and then pushed him off the rocks.

A patterned shape floated towards him, the silver-grey shadow of a fish, the black outline of its eyes, the dark flick of its tail. His heart beat quickly as a circle of gulls rose from the rocks like confetti in the breeze. He couldn't see Ben anywhere, then he saw him near the waves.

He became conscious of the sun and noticed Ben watching the horizon. He looked ghostly, absorbed in the colours and patterns of the sky.

He turned away from him, staring intently at the sea. There was something fanciful about him. He seemed entirely unafraid and focused on the sky.

The waves pummelled his body now, dark shadows drifting, a strange light blurring his vision as he swam towards a figure in the distance. A sea fan fluttered nearby, like a complex network of veins. Dozens of brightly coloured fish scurried past him, the ocean becoming darker as the light disappeared, the swell thrashing his body as water entered his lungs and darkness engulfed him in the waves.

Gasping for breath, he fought his way upwards. He couldn't see Ben anywhere on the sand. Swimming back to the shallows, he glanced up and down the beach and then towards the sandhills. He thought he saw a figure in the distance disappearing with Ben. He remembered his step-father and pulled himself up.

When he reached the sandhills, he saw Ben walking back slowly towards him. He looked frightened.

'What's the matter?'

Ben was staring at him solemnly now.

'What's the matter?' he said impatiently.

'Nothing,' Ben replied coldly.

He wondered what was happening as he glanced down at Ben, who seemed agitated. Did he know anything?

Ben seemed to relax a little and they walked along the sand together to the ocean where he played with him in the waves, hoping to coax an answer from him. He wondered what was wrong with the boy. The idea that he could be gentle with Ben and then brutal in other circumstances troubled and confused him at the same time and he wondered what that meant, whether he was supposed to confess to Benjy's murder, but he knew he would never do that. There would be no confession and he would have to deal with it now in other ways.

Ben held out his hand and when he took it, the boy relaxed a little. Ben let go and he noticed the drifting patterns of clouds in the sky, the same images that Ben had been watching earlier, changing shape and regrouping. He glanced down and saw the seaweed drifting.

When he glanced back, Ben was near the shallows and he knew the boy would lead him to a greater reckoning of what he'd done. It was in the future now and he watched Ben walking towards him from the waves.

The Dark Wood

A road meandered further out of town, houses with motorbikes out front, tipping towards the grass. The houses towards the bush became sparse, overgrown yards with machinery and broken fences.

Simon's place was set back from the road, a trellis of wilting roses over the gate, petals gathered on the ground. I remembered the family next door. It was a rental property and there was always a passing parade of people. The brother had jet-black eyes, high cheekbones, an emaciated body. He used to lie naked on the couch on the front veranda, the faintest of smiles on his lips, a tiny smirk. On another occasion, he locked himself out. He borrowed a ladder and climbed to an upper window. I'd watched, waiting for him to fall.

Simon opened the door when I arrived, and I walked inside. There was a grandfather clock ticking in the back room. His house was cavernous and was on the other side to the family with the boy, the one who climbed to the upper level of the house. The living room had potted plants, tables and chairs, a blue carpet. I wondered if he still saw the boy, if the family were still there. He looked exhausted and picked up a large wine glass. His face was fine-boned, pale skin, a flick of dark hair, delicate lips.

I glanced at a mirror on the wall and then out through the window. There was a sharp drop down into a garden of paths and ferns, bracken and monstera deliciosa. At the bottom, stone steps led down towards a pool and a grotto, a white statue.

When I looked closer, I could see a girl on a swing, ropes hanging from a tree, her long dark dress flicked back with the motion of the swing.

Raindrops blurred the windows. A ghostly haze cloaked plants with thick stems and blood-red flowers. There was a sextant on the table, rusted, an eyeglass and a tangle of metal loops. A wooden chest sat near the corner. When Simon stood up, he opened a slot in the lid, an engraving of a sailing ship inside.

'He drowned at sea, my father. Did I tell you that?'

The loneliness of the ocean, and black water, that's how I remembered it. At the same time, the ocean is a powerful force and Simon's father would be at one with it.

'I've always had a fear of drowning,' he said. 'Even in a swimming pool.'

A certificate hung on the wall, something about marine science. He seemed detached, a little calmer. On each side of the room there were pictures of clippers, wooden masts, and billowing sails. He had them lined up along the sideboard. Near the desk there were ancient maps of the coast, squiggly lines and inlets. Parts of the world were missing or joined together, images of sea monsters rearing their heads, scaled bodies and fins. I glanced over at the wheel and sextant, a guiding instrument, swirls of light in the sky.

He was waiting for me to say something.

'I nearly drowned myself,' he said. 'It was a kind of premonition. I remember losing my depth in the ocean, wanting to sink below the surface. It was relaxing, peaceful. I almost regretted being rescued.'

I stood up and walked to the table, not wanting to say anything. I wondered if he knew about the boy, the one who had also drowned when I should have been watching. It was an odd parallel that both of us had someone who had drowned in our lives. My hands trembled slightly as I touched the edge.

'Well, you'd better show me your books,' I said, changing the subject.

As I glanced at the maps, I imagined the lapping of waves, the movement of a boat, and a black isolation in a watery grave.

There was another table piled high with books. He had his back to me and I studied the bulk of his body, distorted inside his jumper, which had a pattern like knotted rope. When he turned, his eyes were solemn. There were ghostly images on the window panes and I turned back to the books.

Some of them had orange flecks as I flipped the pages quickly, foxing marks from the damp and mould; a number were leather-bound with illustrations and fairy tales – *Alice in Wonderland*, the one with the jabberwocky, and the story of Hansel and Gretel, who were abandoned in the forest. There was a prize for Latin and another one for Ancient History. Where did he get them from?

'I'll give you two hundred dollars for these,' I said, pointing to the ones with fairy tales.

I bundled them up, not sure what he wanted. His dark eyes were probing and I turned away.

There was a sprinkling of stars as I ventured out into the night, not really wanting to return home, remnants of mist, the outlines of a chimney. He gave me the creeps.

Climbing into the car, I turned on the lights, thinking about Simon, something disturbing about him. The lights penetrated the darkness as I turned on the engine, the gentle purr. I thought of Simon back at the house, bent over as if winding down, conserving energy for something important. My hands trembled again, wondering what he was up to. There was a rattle of noise, something in the engine of the car.

A tree towered near the house as I approached. Another tree was uprooted and bending precariously towards the garage. When I walked inside, I noticed a black mark of ash near the fireplace, a circular ring.

I lit the fire and flames leapt up. A plum tree wavered in the wind outside, the circular outline of fruit, clusters of hydrangeas, pink and mauve in the dark.

A branch cracked and I wondered if it was a fox, or the creature that killed a possum in the night. I'd come out in the morning and found the remains, delicate viscera and tufts of fur.

I put paper and wood in a wire holder now, watching the flames. Simon's reclusiveness was bothering me, the fact that he was hiding something. His stories were more elaborate than mine.

There were still tufts of fur on the ground outside in the dark. I could see them near the window. I'd seen it, something obliterated. It was hard to tell what it was. I imagined a killer owl, the span of its wings, swooping down, the shadow against the sky; or maybe a fox, sly and stealthy, slinking towards its prey.

There was a red glow in the distance, the air was icy as I walked outside, and my breath fogged in the night, rasping.

I turned away and walked down the drive. The rain had stopped and I returned to the wood pile to chop more wood, thwacking into it, bringing some into the fire.

Through the window I could see smoke, clouds parting, a pattern of stars. Yesterday I'd walked down to the old house with the pine tree in the yard where the boy used to live but there were only cobwebs in the trees. The boy had drowned in the ocean. I should have been watching but I'd turned away.

There was a knock at the door, and when I opened it, Vince, my friend, was standing there with a young woman. She had arched eyebrows and high cheekbones, wide dark eyes, hair pulled into a ponytail on top of her head. She looked familiar, the same age as the boy if he were alive today.

Vince was wearing a cowboy hat and high-heeled snakeskin boots. His hair straggled to his shoulders. 'Heather, this is Dahlia,' he said.

I wondered what Vince was doing with a girl like this but then I remembered what he was like. He was wearing a large coat, pulled around him to protect from the cold. I ushered them inside.

Vince seemed different to the person I knew years ago, curled back in the shadows towards the fire, watching me, more suspicious.

I began flipping through one of Simon's books, a story called *The Dark Wood*. The first sentence was 'You have to go around the wood, rather than charging through it.' I repeated it slowly to myself.

Hail thundered against the walls in the darkness, the creaking of trees. Dense bush encroached beyond the gardens out back that linked around to Simon's place. Everything led back to Simon's place.

The room was dark and musty. Vince was sitting close to some timber. He had the same lanky body. I remembered the drawing of the ocean at Simon's, creatures emerging from the depths, fish with gaping mouths and sea monsters with sharp spines. Vince picked up the poker and fiddled with it. His dark cowlick was flicked back from the top of his head.

'All this stuff about his father who drowned,' he said. 'Simon, I mean, and then he talks a lot about the lighthouse. He's playing a cat and mouse game with you, Heather. It sounds like you're trying to confuse him but I think he knows what happened.'

I stared at Vince, realising he was referring to the boy, the one who had drowned when I should have been watching. I remembered walking down the street towards the blue mist and a deep drop, a valley stretching wide, the river winding around a curve.

Lights flickered and everything was silent. I sat there in the darkness, listening to the hail hitting the walls and the cracking of lightening. In the darkness, I could see Vince clearly, his thin body, and an image of the boy in the ocean.

I reached over to *The Dark Wood*, flipping through the pages, thinking about the boy, how he'd called out to me, his voice distant. I stared back at Vince and he smiled at me as the gate slammed, ripped away by the violent wind.

*

A shred of curtain brushed the glass and timber had fallen off near the fireplace. It was morning now. I put paper and wood in the fireplace to create a fire, mauve hydrangeas outside. Some people say mauve is a sad colour, fading like twilight but I don't agree.

There were purple vincus plants outside nestled like fallen crosses in thickets of leaves. I walked out and began clearing them away, the continual need to do penance. Cutting away thick stems like twisted rope, I scratched my hands. I stared at the blood as I wrenched them from the soil, heavy against my palms. Tucked away near the fence, tiny pointed leaves of holly were nestled amongst weeds, shadows cast on the wood.

The wind was still high and the track dipped behind the fence into a valley, a dark cliff looming behind the trees. The porch light illuminated the garden. I'd forgotten to turn it off. Two days ago in the dead of night, I'd heard something. It was before midnight and my heart had beaten quickly. I'd noticed rubbish out the front, a tea light on the doorstep as if someone was purifying the place, the light flickering. The objects must have been placed there just before dawn. There had been several instances now when things didn't make sense; a man who had threatened me about the dogs. He'd come at me swearing and I'd felt my heart pounding, but it wasn't him who'd put the tea light and rubbish on the doorstep. Was it someone who knew the boy?

Dark ridges were etched against a sweeping sky, something was coming for me, something watching me. The branches of a tree were pressed up against the glass. I remembered climbing to the top of the tree years earlier before I'd left.

It made me uneasy thinking about it all, the water drifting, blurry images, the boy sinking below the surface. I hadn't been able to reach him in time. What was it that Simon knew? Something coincidental in our lives? He'd said something about his past, that he'd been burdened with guilt.

Inside, the room was dark. Shadowy tendrils brushed the windows. I walked to the wood pile now, striking the wood hard with an axe, bringing some in to fuel the fire. Through the window, I could see smoke next door, clouds parting, a blue sky. People were rising for the new day.

Tomorrow I would walk down to the old house again where I'd lived with my mother and where I'd met the boy's family. I went there every day now.

'You don't belong here,' someone had said. 'You should leave.'

I thought of Simon again. Yesterday there was a dead bird on the ground, perfect as if asleep, a brilliant green and orange. The plum tree in the centre of the yard would be ripe soon with golden fruit dropping to the ground. A cockatoo stared down at me with an amused beady-eyed look.

I'd seen the dead bird on the ground. All these dying creatures on the lawn. I walked out and stood near the trees, watching the long path to the bush. My heart beat quickly again, wanting to do penance, remembering the waves in the ocean, the boy calling out to me, an entranceway of light.

Travelling Through the Fog of Night

A stone wall dipped down from the side of the house, wisteria vine burrowing into the crevices, orange and yellow nasturtium plants.

A piece had crumbled away and through a chink in the wall, I could see the family next door, the father sitting under the shade of a tree, branches moving slightly in the wind. In the corner of the yard, there was a swing, a slippery dip and a child standing on the ladder. The mother was sitting nearby, her neck thin against the soft fabric of her dress. She leant forward, watching the children. Mum was friendly with them and she'd given Heather, the mother, some of her clothes, low-cut tops and shimmery dresses.

I shifted my position and stared up at the house, two-storey, a witch's house, a large grey facade with upper windows, three round porticos at the entrance. There'd been a succession of renters, a family with eleven children, and then a reclusive elderly couple who kept to themselves. Out front, there was another wall that led from the lawn to an enclosed balcony. The house was dark, piles of clothes everywhere, sheets of paper. Heather's baby was usually plonked on the floor, the dog sitting nearby. Out back, the garden was a thicket of weeds. The family usually congregated under a scraggly wisteria vine when the father came to visit. He and Heather had been divorced for some time.

Out front, a group of boys stood near the corner. I recognised them from school. One of them had a freckled face, which lent him a youthful air, a tall physique and intelligent eyes.

Walking back, I noticed the chink in the wall again, the large grey facade forbidding, a crumbling of the boundaries between their world and ours.

There was a loose paling that was propped up against the fence at the back and I walked towards it, feeling a compulsion to get away. The gap was too narrow to climb through, so I grabbed the paling and hauled myself over the fence into the yard next door. Blood dripped slowly towards my sock from a scratch.

I began walking through people's houses and yards. It was a type of mastery of the neighbourhood. I did it all the time, climbing over fences, walking through yards, and then, if I felt like it, through the houses too.

The first fence was wire with a wooden frame and I scaled it easily. I walked up to the house which had an open door. The drone of a TV could be heard down the corridor. There was an eerie silence as I walked along the hallway against the wall, until I reached a TV room out back. The backs of two people were visible, slouched on the couch. The noise from the television drowned out my footsteps now as I slid by towards the door at the side.

Walking out into the garden, I breathed a sigh of relief and confronted another fence, this time a wooden one that was higher. I shimmied up and then over the fence into another yard. I repeated this for several kilometres until I reached the other side of the suburb.

When I arrived back home, the front yard was wide with rhododendrons and wisteria. A group of people were by the side of the road, a suspicious man loitering near the bus stop. He was wearing shorts, legs scaly with eczema. He told me he used to live on the coast and was now living in a caravan park.

I heard a child's cry in the distance. Out front, Heather lifted her toddler on her hip. The child struggled and she put him down. I walked back inside and lay down, listening to the sound of music drifting from Heather's place. Her boyfriend was a saxophone player. He wandered around the neighbourhood with a dazed look and Mum warned me to stay away as he was a heroin addict. He was tall and emaciated, dried up like a husk. There was something deathly about him.

Mum had been feuding with them for a while and had been talking about leaving. I walked over to Heather's place with something Mum had given me to return. A shuffling noise drifted from inside as I noticed the pattern of silvery flecks on the steps. The front door was ajar and I pushed it open. Through the back room, I saw Heather, standing with Marty, her boyfriend. There was an aura of filth about him, something animal and cunning. When he turned, I saw his pale face and thin lips.

I gave Heather the plate Mum had given me and she took it, trembling a little. Marty walked up and put his arm around my shoulder. As he leant closer, I felt the tightness of his grasp. Heather seemed frozen, and instead of moving away he squeezed me tighter. He released his grip, chuckling a little. When I turned back, he was grinning at me. I wondered whether to tell Mum but I knew she'd do nothing.

Marty's skin had a greyish tinge, hair dark and straggly. I remembered Mum saying he'd once been handsome. She'd known them both for a while.

Heather's son had come into our place the previous day. He was about three and dressed only in underpants. Opening his hand, he'd revealed a shiny silver coin, his little face proud and happy.

'Where did you get that from, Pete?' Mum asked.

'Marty gave it to me if I beat up Mummy.'

Mum had looked away embarrassed.

'They'd never hit the children,' she said to me later when he'd left. She looked at me as if that would excuse it all.

I left the house feeling angry, and climbed over some more fences through people's backyards. Then I walked back home, still feeling angry, wondering why no one ever did anything. I was conscious that everything was in disrepair at our place, wall hangings, old couches and the ratty dog. Mum had been talking about moving for some time. She felt compromised living next door to Heather and Marty.

Mum was in the kitchen when I returned and I studied her, thinking how she lived in a dream world, unaware half the time of what was happening. She was wearing a dress with a pattern of mauve flowers, a fineness to her face, dark skin, thick dark eyebrows. I thought of her boyfriend, Alex, who seemed more grounded. He had a place on the coast and I remembered the lake where he'd taken us on a boat. He felt even more frustrated with Mum than I did.

There were fierce birds nesting in crevices in the bush nearby, squawks and cries, raindrops everywhere, melted pale. We were in a tiny village here amongst a string of tiny villages and behind that a vast wilderness. Mum told me once that it was known in Aboriginal tradition that you came here to heal but you could only stay for a short while because the energy was too strong. I didn't know if it was true. It was something someone had told her.

'I'd have a gun if I lived further west,' Alex had said.

'Why?' I'd asked.

'Just for safety.'

There was a strange connection between Mum and Alex. I could see it, something to do with things that had been said, or perhaps hoped and wished for. There was a desire for love but they were keeping each other at arm's length. That's how I saw it, an underlying attraction. I could see it between the two of them. They were both wounded spirits. Mum had been in another relationship where there was violence for many years and it had ended badly.

Alex had sent Mum a beautiful card. It was after they'd been together for a while. It was a painting by Chagall of two lovers kissing, floating in the air. It was titled *The Birthday*.

Sometimes I had an image of Mum standing on a bridge, wanting to move forward but she couldn't. She was always hoping and wishing.

A line of pines led down the side of the house in the mist. I walked out to the fence, staring beyond the bush to the distant trees.

*

In the evening, I walked outside again. The moon glowed, pale and white, an aurora of light, like a blue halo. I followed the path into the bush. In the distance, I could see Alex's house amongst the trees and I wondered if we could live at his place on the coast. Alex's house was made of planked wood set back in the forest. Mum still loved him, I was positive. I thought about Alex's comments that we should move to the coast, that it was better there, more open and friendly. Studying the light shining from his window, I walked up to the long veranda around the side, the shapes of the trees, irregular in the dark. They frightened me, glimpses of light between them.

After I knocked, Alex walked out, tall, and slim, grey shaggy hair. I followed him inside and sat down in the corner. Flames licked the side of the fireplace, a crackling sound. Alex's dog was nearby. It had a sleek body and long tail. The sound of the dog panting softly was comforting. In the corner there was a poker for the fire and a book about fishing. Through the window, I noticed a garden Alex had been planting according to the phases of the moon. It was beautiful, the rows of herbs and vegetables.

'Yes, the garden was planted according to the moon,' he'd said the previous week. 'Lettuce, spinach, broccoli. Those are the ones planted with the new moon. Beans, peppers, tomatoes with the second quarter phase of the moon, beets and carrots with the full moon.'

I smiled at him, thinking how he was different to Mum, measured and calm. Mum was reckless and a dreamer. I glanced around at a pile of books, an ashtray. There was a faint residue of tobacco. Outside, I could see the pine trees and the mist.

'I've nearly finished my book,' he said. He was here trying to finish his manuscript about his family who were pioneers in the district.

There were ferns through the window and behind the fence, a gully of bush that stretched away to the town. At night, I could hear the sound of rain against our windows and the trains whooshing in the darkness. Mist rolled across the valley, a clap of thunder and dark shadows, the mist gathering as we travelled through the fog of night.

The Keeper of the Light

A winding staircase led to the upper level of the house, a black marble fireplace, high ceilings, a velveteen couch that looked out onto a sunroom awash with light.

I walked into Mum's room and noticed a photo of Grandma as a stiff-backed little girl on a horse, her gaze commanding. Her father was holding the horse's reins. I never knew him and whenever she spoke of him it was in hushed tones: 'Only the good die young.'

Grandma's father was standing directly in front of her. He had blond hair, blue eyes, like myself, different to Grandma and Mum, who were dark and sultry. Grandma looked more commanding than her father, even at four. There was another picture of him reading in a greenhouse, the sun's rays piercing the glass. He looked relaxed and was bent over the book.

A gauze curtain moved slightly in the wind that whispered through the dandelions and jasmine outside. I could see my sister, Sandy, dangling her legs over the fence, her unruly hair tied into a loose ponytail. Her dress was scruffy and torn, her red sandals the same shade as the ball she was holding. Shifting forward slightly on the fence, she pushed herself off with a springing movement as if nothing could stop her. I left the house and walked to the edge of the path, watching her on the beach. Sandy was with a group of kids on the shoreline, building a sandcastle. A skipping rope lay in the yard with her dolls out along the grass, the plastic cups and saucers from a tea set. Near the tea set, she'd placed an old doll handed down from Mum. It had somehow remained unbroken.

Mum was in the kitchen as I walked back inside. She was speaking in whispers on the phone, talking to her sister Julie about Grandma, who was in a hostel now, what she was going to do about her. Her arm was resting on the chair and her dark sunglasses were pushed back on her head. I had an urge to rip them off because she wore them as a camouflage when she didn't want to talk about things, a kind of shield against trouble.

'What are you doing?' she asked, hanging up the phone.

'Nothing. I was just outside, watching Sandy. I might go out later. I can't stay long.'

Fear flashed across her face, a reaction to uncertainty. I could smell jasmine in the yard through the window. Sandy's tea cups were blown around by the wind on the grass. When I looked back, Mum's gaze was fixed on me.

I left the room and walked back to the living room, lounging back on the couch, watching a game show on TV. Mum had appeared on it once. I was Sandy's age at the time and I'd gone along to the TV studio, excited that Mum was appearing on the game show and that she might win a prize. Sitting in the audience, I was shocked to discover that good-looking actors like Mum were employed to play the part of ordinary people on TV. She was supposed to be a teacher from a suburb in the outer ring but it was a game show not a drama.

'But how can they do that?' I'd asked, completely disillusioned. I was young then and Mum had merely laughed. 'It's a game show, darling, not reality.'

Sandy's teacups were still on the lawn blown into a corner. I looked out the window and saw her appear at the top of the path and rearrange them, carefully placed in a row, fanning outwards. Then she scooped them up in her arms, destroying the pattern of cups like a Buddhist sand mandala, the light on the swimming pool like a luminous sea.

The following day, I drove along the road to Grandma's, wondering what kind of mood she'd be in, as I knew she hated the hostel. She was beautifully dressed and made up when I arrived, linen pants and an elegant top, delicate jewellery. Her hands were resting precariously on the bed and I helped her up. She gripped hold of the walker and steadied herself. I tried to grab hold of her arm but she waved me aside crankily.

'I don't like it here,' she said as we moved slowly along the corridor. 'There's this woman, she dominates the dining table. It's cliquey.'

As she moved along the hallway bent over the walker, I pointed to beautiful paintings on the wall; artwork with bright colours.

Grandma paused and studied them carefully.

'They're lovely paintings, don't you think?' I said. 'I heard you've been painting. Mum said there's a guy who does art classes.'

'Yes, I've been painting,' she replied.

'I saw photos of your artwork,' I said hesitantly.

She murmured something I couldn't hear and pushed herself forward on the walker.

I noticed an elderly woman and man sitting at the entrance. They sat there all day. Grandma didn't like them, felt unnerved by them, said they were the presence of death. They remained there watching and waiting. I glanced at them. They looked like elderly people trapped or bored, nothing sinister. Grandma breathed a sigh of relief as we passed by.

We walked across the car park and climbed into the car and I noticed her look downwards.

'Are you okay?' I asked as her hands trembled slightly.

She bit her lip and I reached over and touched her hand. She gripped my own hand tightly then released it.

'I'm glad you're here,' she said.

I noticed her relax but there was something upsetting her. I could see it in the strained expression in her eyes.

'I wish you could come up more often. You're a bridge between me and your mum and Julie.'

'Yes, I'd like to. I'll come more often. I promise.' I clasped her hand again then released it and started the car.

Grandma turned and gazed out the window.

When we arrived at the surf club, she sat there staring out at the sea. There were crowds of people on the beach.

'I like the light,' she said.

I remembered one of the photos of her paintings Mum had shown me. The light was shimmering on the sea, elusive.

I studied her beautifully made up face, large dark eyes and observed a well of melancholy carefully masked beneath.

'If you lived near me,' she said, 'it would be so much easier to see you. Maybe you could come up and spend more time here.'

'I'll try,' I said. 'I mean it. I'll see what I can do.'

She glanced away from me quickly.

'I'm sorry about Julie taking the car. I can't do anything about it. You know it's between you and Julie and it's probably for the best. You nearly had an accident.'

She glanced downwards again.

'Do you want to come to Julie's tomorrow?' I asked, feeling troubled. 'She'll be gone then. She's away for a couple of weeks. I'm house-minding.'

'That would be nice,' she said tersely.

We chatted about Mum and Julie.

'The problem with your mother,' she said, 'is that when she's upset she becomes a hot angry person and when Julie's upset, she's a cold angry person, so there's no communication.'

'Yeah, you're right,' I said.

'I don't understand it,' she replied, as if it were a mystery. 'Different personalities, too close together in age, but I was so nervous with your mother. I had no experience, you see. I was an only child and I decided I had to have another child quickly. It wasn't good. I don't know, I did my best but I failed.' She lowered her head slightly.

'They love you. It doesn't matter,' I replied.

She glanced up at me, then away towards the sea.

'How did you go?' Mum asked when I rang that night from Julie's. 'She's so difficult, isn't she?'

'She's very frail. She definitely doesn't like the hostel. There's these continual flashes of anger and sadness. I think you should see her more.'

There was silence on the end of the phone.

'Are you enjoying staying at Julie's?'

'It's okay here. I'm driving Grandma up here tomorrow. Julie's gone now.'

'Good idea. Give her a change of scene.'

I hung up, bothered by Mum's distance, her unpleasant tone, as if she were punishing Grandma. I remembered her saying it was a joke that Grandma complained about the hostel when she'd told Mum as a child at boarding school to toughen up if she ever had problems.

'She had no sympathy,' she said. 'She was cold and unfeeling. You don't know what it was like having her as a mother.'

In the morning when I drove Grandma up to Julie's, she paced on her walker, commenting how she didn't like it there. I could see she was taking charge, trying to assert herself, making an assessment of Julie's life.

'It has a bad atmosphere here,' she commented.

She must have been thinking about Julie's ex, who she was upset with.

'This is the nicest room in the house,' she said, walking into the study. 'Don't you think so, Polly?'

She was right; the rest of the house could be dark. It was particularly unnerving at night, the darkness and high rafters, the distant shapes of the plants outside brushing up against the walls, and the clacking of the wind chime outside. It had driven me mad in the night. I'd gone out and taped it up as it sounded like a mournful dog baying in the distance.

'The place has an unpleasant feeling,' Grandma said, echoing my thoughts. 'I don't like it any more. I can sense Malcolm's presence.'

'Really?' I asked. 'You sense his presence?'

'Yes, I don't know, just a feeling like, you know, he's still around.'

The place did have a strange feeling, Malcolm, Julie's ex, had done annoying impractical things like alter the garage door so it didn't open properly. There were dozens of shoes in Julie's wardrobe, pencil holders full of pens. It was as if he'd marked his territory.

'Do you want to go for a drive? We can go and see Julie's friend Veronica. You always liked her. Maybe it'll be good to get away.'

She nodded and I helped her collect her things, then we walked slowly to the car.

The road dipped towards the sea, a glittering mosaic of light. Vero's place was against the hill. The original garden had been razed to the ground. I could see Grandma's mood shift to one of excitement and expectation as we drove up towards the door.

Glancing towards the headland, I helped Grandma out of the car and we walked slowly towards the entrance where I rang the bell.

'Come in,' Vero said, smiling, as she opened the door to us. 'I haven't seen you for ages.'

She sat down opposite in the living room, her long legs tanned by the sun. Her smile revealed front teeth with a small gap that gave her a mischievous air. There was a boundless energy about her and every so often she turned her head a little and looked at me from a slightly side on angle as if she were only too aware of the friction in the family. I could see the lamp glinting now. The sun hit the window, a half eaten meal on the table.

Grandma looked uneasy.

'Are you still seeing Leo?' Vero asked me.

'Leo?' I said. There seemed to be an underlying purpose behind the question. 'No, we're just friends. It was always just friends.'

'Just as well,' Grandma snapped.

I was surprised by the bitter tone in her voice and wondered if she was being ironic.

'Why do you say that? He's funny.'

'Funny? He's a womaniser.'

Leo was an actor like Mum, a friend of the family. He had green eyes, heavy build, and a broad handsome face. I could tell from Grandma's expression she didn't like him, had probably never liked him. I noticed her posture stiffen.

'He's not the sort of man anyone should take seriously,' Grandma said.

I bit my lip, observing her angry reaction.

'It's more than that,' she added. 'He's someone to avoid, Polly. I've been wanting to say something about it for some time. You don't know him. He has another side.'

I stared at her, wondering what she meant. In our family, women had been done over by charming womanisers and it was clear she didn't want another generation affected by it. I glanced at Vero, knowing she knew Leo too and that was why Grandma was raising it. Vero didn't take Leo seriously either, but then both she and Grandma liked younger men. Leo was older than me but surely he was too young for Grandma. I looked at her dark eyes and high cheekbones, the carefully sculptured hair. She was very beautiful when she was young.

I remembered going to Leo's flat, the well appointed view, the tree-lined street, and then standing in the living room as he started talking to me about art. He was funny and interesting. He knew I was studying art and wanted to show me some paintings. He'd worked with Mum and I'd been interested in acting myself.

Grandma cast a disapproving eye over my appearance and I was conscious that I looked dishevelled, had put on weight, my jeans and top were a little too tight. While at twice my age, Vero was slim and well-dressed in a short dress that showed off her legs, fashionable shoes, and Grandma, who was four times my age, was also elegantly dressed. I knew, though, that like Mum, Grandma maintained an appearance, a type of mask that kept trouble at bay, one which never revealed her true feelings.

Almost unconsciously, I started talking about the painting I'd been doing at uni, how it was my own way of making sense of the world. It seemed to be safer ground.

The room had a faint odour of perfume, a cabinet of drinks and a bar in the corner. Vero always liked observing my family. I noticed her smiling at me now. I could almost hear her thoughts.

Vero pointed to a mirror on the wall. 'Leo gave it to me,' she said provocatively. It was as if she were testing Grandma.

Grandma flinched when she said his name. 'Really?' she said sarcastically.

'I don't know why you don't like Leo, Barbara. I thought you were hard on him. I mean he had a terrible childhood. You know that.'

I sat up straight now, remembering Leo telling me he'd been bullied relentlessly and that his father had been an alcoholic. There was a type of anxiety with him that made him want to accelerate the relationship as quickly as possible, get the worst out of the way, or the most shameful. I didn't think he was interested in me at all, I was too young. We were just friends.

Grandma glanced down at the floor and I wondered if there was more to it. She could be hard on people, intolerant. What sort of things had happened in her own childhood? She could meddle; tell lies too if it suited her. Maybe she'd made it up.

'He goes out with as many women as possible to maximise his chances,' she said. 'Spreading the net. My grandfather was like that. He was a brutal man. It had a bad effect on my mother.'

I glanced at her, surprised. This must be why she hadn't taken to motherhood herself. She said nothing further, changed the subject abruptly, and we chatted about Vero's work as a teacher.

In the late afternoon, I drove Grandma back and she glanced at me with that melancholy expression again. I glanced back at her and could tell she didn't want to talk about things.

'I'll be back soon,' I said. 'Don't worry.'

She studied me in a resigned way and, feeling troubled, I kissed her goodbye.

I drove to Mum's place and walked down to my room. There was a labyrinth of many rooms in the house, a garden out back with palm trees and frangipani.

Mum was in the kitchen and I walked down the hall. She looked at me warily when I walked in.

'Grandma was talking about her childhood and her grandfather. It sounded bad. She really hates Leo, you know.'

Mum looked away. 'I don't know anything about her grandfather. As for Leo, it's obvious what he's like.'

'Why don't you know anything about her grandfather?'

She shrugged. 'She never talks about it. It was just her way of coping with things, stiff upper lip.'

'What about Leo?'

'I don't know. He had a sad background but he manipulates you with it. When I met him, I was younger than you. I was only fifteen.'

'Fifteen? I didn't realise you were that young.'

'Grandma didn't like it. She warned him off, confronted him.'

'So she tried to protect you. You said she never protected you.'

'It's not black and white with her.'

She stared back at me and seemed tense now as she offered me some tea. She poured the amber liquid out into the cup. There were chocolates and slices. Picking one up, she bit into it, looking irritated. For Mum, it was all part and parcel of experience.

'I think Grandma might have to go to a nursing home,' she said.

'Why? She's sharp as a tack.'

'She's quite ill, Polly. You don't understand, it's her heart. I don't think she can go on much longer. She's worn out. You've been unaware of things.'

I could smell jasmine in the yard again, knowing Mum was hitting back at me, and through the window outside the gardener worked amongst the plants.

'I still don't understand about Leo,' I said angrily.

'Well, something happened to Grandma when she was young. Best to leave it, Polly.'

'What?'

'I don't know. It was a long time ago now. She never talks about it.'

When I looked up, Mum was leaning back in the chair, her arm resting on the side. Her sunglasses were perched on top of her head again and I waited to see if she pulled them down over her eyes but she didn't.

She was frowning at me as if I were becoming a nuisance. The previous week, I'd overheard her talking about me to Greg, her partner, in a detached cold tone as if I were naive and blundered into things. I studied her and she looked pensive. Sandy had told me Mum had said jokingly once, 'Polly doesn't play the game.'

Sometimes, I saw Mum in the kitchen working on a dinner party before she made herself glamorous for the evening, completely unaware of what Sandy and I were doing. It was like a facade, the glamour and distraction. Greg was mean with money unless it came to entertainment, where he liked to indulge himself and came into his own. When you questioned him or stepped on his neuroses, he became aggressive and commanding but then when things were personalised he withdrew, lost trust and became suspicious.

Sandy walked into the room. She looked nervous and a sense of panic set in, knowing she'd be left alone here with them when I was gone. She was still protected, though, the youngest child, but that would change. All the confidence I'd seen earlier in her would disintegrate. Patterns barely registered with her, just a world of fantasy and playacting, but soon it would be her turn. I stared at her pityingly.

Sandy was waiting for me to say something, trying to gauge how she should react.

The light shone through the window and I saw palm trees in the distance and the path to the beach. I remembered Grandma on the balcony at the surf club, how she'd looked contemplative as if she were planning something.

The humidity was intense and when I walked outside in the evening, a myriad of stars shone in the sky, silence, a car whizzing past, a heavy feeling around the mountain. Julie said there was a fire last season. They could see flames in the darkness like a volcano, a dotted trail of light leading to the summit, jets of fire. There was a sense of escape, a wild beginning.

When I reached the path at the top of the garden that led to the beach, Sandy's teacups were sitting precariously on the grass. I picked them up and rearranged them. Sandy was the one I spoke to the most, not the others. I hardly spoke to Dad. In fact, I never saw him and when I did, I hardly said anything.

Walking down to the beach, I saw a boat in the distance. People were grouped together on the sand. I followed another trail through the bush, leaves strewn across the ground, stone steps with moss covering the edges. There was something on the ground, metallic with a green sheen, an old piece of metal, shiny, a flick of greenery. A motorbike was hidden in the bushes. I could see the black outline, cicadas humming. The house was set back in the lee of the mountain. When I looked up, Grandma was sitting on the veranda, staring out across the trees, studying the horizon, looking away.

She was leaning back in the chair and turned to face me, sitting up tensely when I arrived. 'I was just thinking about things,' she said. 'I borrowed a friend's car and drove here.'

'What were you thinking?'

'Just that you should keep your own counsel, Polly. Don't get caught up in all this. I understand where you're coming from. There's been too much deception in the family. Sometimes people need illusions to cope, but you're not like that.'

I reached over and clutched her hand. She squeezed my own hand tightly, glancing up. The paintings she'd been doing back at the hostel were important to her, I could tell, those beautiful images of light.

'Did you see the fire on the mountain? Julie told me about it.'

'Yes, I did,' she said. 'It burnt slowly towards the summit.'

She looked away from me.

I glanced at the winding staircase that led down to the lower level of the house. Mum was downstairs and I walked down below. She was in the kitchen. I remembered the game show she'd appeared on. It was a type of deflection from reality; the world of acting was an escape, something that helped her process things, but sometimes the line between fiction and reality became blurred. Grandma was right, I wasn't like that. For me, it was always important to get to the emotional truth of the matter.

The light shone through the palm trees and I could see the path to the beach that disappeared into the night. A moth flittered by and I caught it in my hand. When I looked up, Grandma walked in. She smiled at me, her eyes intent and steady as she sat down next to me, the keeper of the light.

www.ingramcontent.com/pod-product-compliance
Lightning Source LLC
Chambersburg PA
CBHW030215130726
47898CB00012B/1033